TORNADIC

TAMI BRUMBAUGH

ISBN-13: 978-1945634048
ISBN: 1945634049

To Pete,
Continually drawn to tornadoes
like a moth to a flame
Maybe that's why Kansas
has sucked you in

CONTENTS

CHAPTER 1

MISCHIEVOUS WIND

A mischievous wind howled and whistled as it shook the house. It tormented the budding limbs of a maple tree, forcing them to scrape the house's taupe siding.

Brayden cringed and cranked up his music. They had a tree pruner. Why hadn't Dad clipped the branches? If he complained, his mom would tell *him* to do it.

"You're sixteen years old. It's time for you to help out around here," she would say.

It was better to keep quiet. He pressed his forehead to the cool window pane and watched the wind continue to harass the tree. A white plastic bag clung to the lowest branch until a wicked gust tore it free, tossing it back and forth. Brayden shrugged. Wind in Kansas. Nothing new.

He yanked more dirty clothes out from under his bed. It was laundry day, and his mom only washed clothes that were in the hamper. He came across three folded t-shirts. Had he put away the clean clothes from last week? Probably not, but it was too late now. They were dirty by association and might as well get washed again. Random socks hugged the wall. Brayden grabbed a gray one and sniffed it. He gagged and threw the entire heap into the hamper and rolled it out the door. Time to relax.

His iPhone was charging on his dresser. He grabbed it, stuck in some ear buds, and sprawled out on his bed. Soon he was sucked into a new game featuring zombies.

A pale hand grabbed his arm. Brayden jolted out of bed. The hand was attached to his ten-year-old sister, Willow, standing innocently in front of him. Brayden yanked out his ear buds.

"Don't you ever knock?" he demanded.

"I *did* knock. You just didn't answer."

"Then you should have left."

"But I wanted to give you this." She pulled a jumble of plastic, sticks, and string out from behind her back.

Brayden squinted. "What is that?"

"Can't you tell?" She held the creation up to his face.

"Still no clue."

Willow sat on the floor and positioned two triangular yellow objects side by side. "They're kites!"

"If you say so."

"I cut up an old plastic table cloth and taped it to some sticks. Mom gave me lots of string, so I could make a kite for each of us. Can you tell which one is for you?"

One kite was filled with pink, purple, and green butterflies. The other had footballs and a strange spotted shape with eyes.

"I'm guessing mine is the one with mud clumps and the moldy burrito."

Willow's smile faded. "It's supposed to be footballs and your leopard gecko. I never tried drawing a gecko before. It was kind of tricky. I just wanted to draw stuff you might like."

8

"Great. You can leave it on the floor if you want." He turned back to his game. "Close the door on your way out."

She didn't move.

"Oh. Yeah. Thanks for the kite." He rolled over.

She crossed her arms. "But it's windy outside."

"And?"

"And it's a Saturday."

"So?"

"I thought we could go fly the kites now."

Brayden grimaced. "I don't really fly kites anymore."

"Because all of your old kites are torn up. Now you have a new kite. The string isn't tangled. It should work great."

"Even a new kite-type-object isn't my thing. High Schoolers don't play with kites."

"Says who?" she asked.

"Everyone in high school. Why don't you ask a little neighbor kid to fly kites with you?"

Willow's shoulders slumped. "Because I made the kite special for you." She picked up the string from her kite and dragged the plastic triangle out of his room.

Brayden rolled back over on his bed and renewed his focus on his video game. He could hear the kite thumping down the stairs. The front door opened and slammed shut. He stuck in the ear buds and fought more digital zombies, but his eyes strayed to the rejected kite on the floor.

During a third game, his score took a nosedive. He shoved his straight, caramel hair off his forehead in frustration and glanced back at the abandoned kite.

With a sigh of exasperation, he grabbed the kite by the gecko tail and stomped down the stairs. He could only take so much guilt.

Willow was running down the sidewalk in front of their house. Her flower kite flopped on the ground behind her.

She frowned, brushed off the kite, and began sprinting in the opposite direction. Once again, the kite merely bumped along, finally landing in a clump of dandelions. Her wispy blond hair whipped around her face while her skinny arms held the kite string high in the air.

Brayden shook his head, dropped his kite to the ground, and walked towards her. "Wait! I'll hold the kite up while you start running."

Willow stopped and turned toward him. "I thought you were *too old* to fly kites."

He shrugged. "I'm not too old to help you."

Her face lit up with a smile. "Okay." She handed him her kite and started to walk away.

Brayden thrust the kite into the air. "Run!"

Willow's scrawny legs pumped hard as she tore down the sidewalk. The string stretched and Brayden released the kite. It soared and dipped and then plummeted to the ground.

"Stop!" he yelled. "You almost had it. Let's try again."

Willow waited for his command and then bolted. This time the kite stayed in the air.

"Turn around!" Brayden called.

She spun around and squealed, holding tightly to the kite string. "It's working! My flowers are flying!"

The wind rustled the new blades of grass on either side of the sidewalk. It gently swayed the trees, content now that it had the pleasure of floating a kite.

Brayden soaked in her delight. He looked up and down the street. They were all alone. No kids played outside their homes. Cars were still parked cozily in their garages. He walked back to the house and picked up his kite. After a second scan down the street, he began to run until his kite climbed into the air. He hated to admit it, but this was actually fun.

"Yeah!" Willow yelled. Her neon pink panda shirt flapped in the wind.

When was the last time he had seen his sister this happy? His big-brother job description usually included tormenting her, but for this moment it was great knowing he was part of her happiness. Of course, he couldn't be kind for *too* long.

"Careful, runt. You're so scrawny the wind may just blow you higher than your kite."

Willow giggled. "Then you'd better fly with your kite and save me."

"I suppose," Brayden said, grinning.

He watched her release more string as her kite soared and dipped in the fickle wind. Her light blue eyes and fragile freckled face looked back at him. Her mouth stretched into a huge smile.

That smile etched itself into his mind, haunting and bringing him relief in the days to come.

When the wind fizzled, Brayden reluctantly returned to his room and began his math assignment. Algebra II was a decent class, but he was burned out. One more month of school. He couldn't wait for the year to end. He focused long enough to complete the problems on the front page, but struggled to finish the back.

"Dinner!" Mom called.

Brayden dropped his pencil, grateful for a break. He charged out of his room and nearly tripped over his sister and their tri-colored beagle, Banjo. "What are you doing?"

Willow was sprawled out on her stomach across the tan carpet with her bare feet crossed in the air. She had her thick purple notebook open, and a stubby pencil in her hand that she used to write with loopy letters.

She glanced at him. "I'm writing a story."

Brayden looked over her shoulder. On the top of the page, she had used markers to draw a picture of two mice flying kites. One mouse was wearing a neon pink panda shirt.

"What's the story about?"

She flipped back to the cover of her notebook and pointed to the black puffy letters spelling *PRIVATE COLLECTION*. "That's for me to know and you to never find out." She turned back to the kite story and began writing again.

"Mom called us for dinner," Brayden said.

"I'll be right there. I'm in my groove."

"Fine, but don't get mad if I eat it all."

Brayden continued downstairs and inspected the meal. There was chicken with black and green spices flecked over the top, a heaping bowl of brown rice, and a smaller bowl with suspicious-looking green ovals. Each dish perched on floral hot pads.

His dad joined him at the table while his mom finished pouring water into their glasses.

"What are the weird green things?" Brayden asked, pointing to the unfamiliar food.

"Edamame," Mom stated.

"Eda-what-what?"

"Edamame," Mom repeated. "I'm trying something new. It's supposed to be good for us."

"Great." He pushed the vegetable farther away.

"We're going to support your mom and try it," Dad said with a forced smile.

"Where's your sister?" Mom asked.

"Writing in the hallway."

"Willow! We're eating!" Dad called.

Willow approached the table supporting her notebook with one hand and still writing. She sat down and placed the notebook on her plate.

"Would you like me to serve rice on your mice pictures?" asked Dad.

"I'm almost done."

The rest of the family heaped food on their plates. Willow wrote "The End" and dropped her notebook on the floor. The story was exposed, so she leaned over to flip the cover back into place. Mom prayed and they started eating.

"What's the green stuff?" Willow asked.

"Edamame," Mom said again.

Willow plucked one bean out of the bowl and popped it into her mouth. She chewed slowly. "Not bad." She dumped a large serving onto her plate.

Dad and Brayden looked at each other and stabbed a few beans with their forks. They hesitantly stuck the food in their mouth at the same time and chewed. Brayden grimaced. Dad quickly washed it down with water.

"Oh, come on," said Mom. "It's not that bad."

Dad scooted the bowl closer to Mom. "I'm glad you like it. You're welcome to finish it off."

"Someday I'm going to find something healthy that all of you will actually eat."

"We're eating the brown rice," said Brayden with a sheepish grin. "You said that was healthy."

"I suppose. It's a start, anyhow." Mom's smile returned. "I saw both of you kids—"

"Teen and kid," Brayden corrected.

"—out there flying kites," Mom finished. "That looked like fun."

"It was GREAT!" Willow exclaimed. "Brayden helped me get mine in the air and it stayed up for a super long time. He even flew *his* kite!"

"I noticed that," Mom said. "I couldn't resist taking a picture. I can't remember the last time Brayden flew a kite."

"Yeah. Well, the moldy burrito almost looked like my gecko up in the sky."

"Very funny." Willow turned to Dad. "See. You're always grumbling about the wind. At least it's great for flying kites."

"Good to hear. I guess I'll let it keep blowing for a few more days. As long as I can get Brayden to clip the branches off our maple tree. The limbs are going to scrape the paint off our house some day."

Brayden's rice fell off his fork. So much for not complaining.

CHAPTER 2

VANISHING CLOUDS

Four days passed, and Brayden had yet to clip the maple tree branches. His excuse Sunday was that they had church and it was a day of rest. The following three days, it was rainy and he had homework to complete after school.

Today could be a problem. He slouched in his chair and stared out the smudged window. The clouds were gone and the sun beamed, eager to warm people once again. It was third hour English class already, and so far none of the teachers had decided to give homework.

Mr. Hankenson paced back and forth as he discussed scenes from *A Separate Peace*. Brayden yawned. He read the first few chapters last week, but knew he was behind. Was it worth catching up if it meant avoiding tree pruning another day? How much reading would he have to do?

He glanced around the class, searching for someone who would know what chapter the class was on. Maddie and Sophie were passing notes, and probably hadn't read anything. Connor was a reliable source, but his head was in his arms and he was snoring peacefully.

Maybe he still had a reading schedule somewhere in his own notebook. He searched his crinkled pages until Trey elbowed him and pointed to his right. Several of his football buddies were snickering. When they caught Brayden's eye, they pointed in the same direction.

Logan was the object of their scorn. He was hunched over his paper, furiously taking notes. His glasses were askew and his brown hair was parted down the middle, revealing a stubborn cowlick in back. His gray corduroy pants were several inches too short and revealed long white tube socks. Three spitballs were lodged in his hair; one rested on his shoulder and two stuck to his shirt collar.

Trey grinned, and plucked another spitball from his mouth. He positioned it on his notebook and flicked it. The sopping wad of paper bounced off Logan's shirt. The guys smirked.

Trey nudged Brayden. "See if you can make it stick," he whispered.

Brayden wasn't in the mood, but knew the guys expected him to join in the fun. He tore off a scrap of paper and chewed it. Mr. Hankenson was writing on the dry erase board, oblivious to the competition behind him. With a good flick, Brayden sent the spitball flying. It struck Logan's neck and rolled into his collar. The guys gave a silent cheer.

"Why was Gene jealous of Finny?" asked Mr. Hankenson.

Logan raised his hand. The spitballs lodged in his collar rolled down his shirt. The boys tried to stifle their laughter.

"Is something funny, gentlemen?"

They each shook their head.

"How about one of you answers the question. Brayden?"

Brayden felt his face flush. Had he read far enough? "Because...Finny was better at doing stuff?"

"True, but let's be more specific. Trey?"

"He was better at...football?" Trey guessed. He rubbed his recently shaved head. Trey was one of the few guys that looked good without hair. He bore a striking resemblance to a young Michael Jordan.

Mr. Hankenson sighed. "Try reading next time. Logan?"

"Gene was jealous of Finny's athletic ability, especially when he broke a swimming record on his first try. He was also jealous of Finny's charisma that allowed him to get away with things." Logan brushed the spitballs out of his hair and looked accusingly at Brayden and his football friends.

The bell rang. Students gathered their books and crammed out the door. Trey and the spitball crew began laughing out loud.

Max pounded Brayden on the back. "Did you see the evil eye Logan gave us? Should we be scared?"

Trey laughed. "We'd better use the buddy system in case he tries to beat us up."

The halls were congested with students rushing to their lockers. Brayden and his friends strutted down the middle of the hall. He felt a surge of power as the masses parted before them. It was like a blast of wind blew people out of the way. In the upper classman hall this was not always the case, but in a few years, even that would not be a problem.

Brayden already had his Algebra II book, so he sauntered straight to class, fist bumping his group as they meandered to other rooms. He pulled out his completed assignment, and kicked back in his desk.

Did his power stem from being on the football team? That probably helped. He wasn't exactly a star player, but he worked hard in practices and held his own. Most of his game time was spent on the bench. But that should change

17

next year when he was a junior. He liked to think most of his power came from his confidence and sense of humor. He glanced at his reflection in the window. Maybe he wasn't that bad looking either. His face wasn't covered in zits like some of the guys, and he didn't have a huge nose or bulging Adam's apple. His mom always said she loved his sparkling brown eyes. Of course, moms were biased. He stroked his chin. Yeah, not too bad.

"Feeling full of yourself, huh?"

Brayden twisted around in his chair. Kenzie Winslow.

She rolled her eyes. "And here I thought you were just arrogant when you were with your football buddies. Should I get a mirror for you so you can get a better view?"

"Nah. A mirror can't contain my awesomeness." He smiled at her.

The guys next to him laughed. Kenzie did not.

"Are you having a rough morning?" Brayden asked.

"Actually, my morning is just fine. I wonder if Logan can say the same. Seems like being a spitball target might not make for a great start to the day."

"Oh, come on. Spitballs don't hurt." Brayden handed her a piece of paper. "Would you like to throw some at me? I can take it."

"It's not the same thing."

"Take your seat, class," Mrs. Brinkhaus said.

Kenzie cast one more look of disdain at Brayden and sat two rows away.

Brayden kept a cocky smile on his face, but he was troubled by Kenzie's obvious dislike for him. Who did she think she was calling him out like that? Several girls gathered around her and began an animated discussion. Why did so many people like her?

"Exchange your homework," instructed Mrs. Brinkhaus. "We'll check your answers and see if you have any questions."

Brayden traded papers with the guy next to him. He absentmindedly checked off answers that differed from what the teacher wrote on the board. His eyes strayed to Kenzie. Her wavy black hair cascaded down to her waist and obscured most of her face. They finished grading papers and passed them back. Kenzie turned to smile at her friend. She never smiled at him. She was actually very pretty when she wasn't frowning. But she was also pretty annoying.

Kenzie caught him looking at her and rolled her big blue eyes. He scowled. Everyone liked him. Why didn't she know that? Didn't she watch how other students treated him? He was respected.

"Your new assignment is on the board. We'll go over the first two questions together, and then I'll give you some time to work on your own. Maya, put the snack away. You can wait until lunch."

Maya blushed and shoved an opened bag of Doritos into her backpack. She wiped her chubby orange fingers on her jeans. The guy sitting beside her puffed out his cheeks and imitated her eating. Several classmates laughed. Kenzie glared at them and gave Maya a sympathetic smile. Brayden was glad he had managed not to laugh. Kenzie probably would have clawed him.

Time ticked by slowly as the class scribbled down math problems. A sigh of relief escaped several students when the bell rang. Kenzie walked out with her friends without giving him a second glance. Brayden shook his head. Why did he even care?

Trey met him at his locker. "I'm starving. There had better be some good food left. Let's go."

19

Brayden fumbled with the lock and tossed his books inside. They strutted to the lunchroom. Max and the guys were already spread out at their table. They shoved their food over to make room for Brayden and Trey.

Max stuffed half of his hamburger into his mouth and began to chew. "Nineteen and a half days left of school," he announced.

"And then what?" asked Ian. "Are you just going to laze around at home again?"

"Nope." A chunk of chewed hamburger dropped out of Max's mouth. "I'm going to get me a job this time."

Trey chuckled. "Doing what? Nobody would want to hire you."

"You could be part of Three Hunks and a Truck Moving Company," Brayden suggested. "Oh, wait. You aren't a hunk and you don't have a truck."

"You are mistaken there, my friend." Max ran his fingers through his thick, black hair. "I'm both good-looking *and* my dad now has a truck."

"Which he would be crazy to let you drive," added Trey.

"You could hold up a sign on the street corner, advertising pizza," said Parker. "I'm sure that pays a lot."

Max gave a hoot with his mouth still full. This time a french fry fell out.

"You could teach little kids a class on manners," said Brayden. "Your etiquette is clearly a great example."

"*Etiquette*? Maybe *you* could teach kids how to use big words," Ian said.

The guys laughed. Max finally swallowed. "Okay. You guys are so full of great ideas. What are *you* going to do this summer?"

"I'm going to hang out at the neighborhood pool. That way all the girls can admire my muscles," said Gavin.

"What muscles?" asked Parker.

"These muscles." Gavin grabbed Parker in a head lock.

"I know what Brayden is going to do this summer," said Ian in a sugary voice. "He's going to fly kites every day with his sister."

Brayden's jaw dropped. "How did you..."

"Your mom was talking to my mom. They both thought it was so sweet. The rest of the day, my mom lectured me on treating my little brother and sister better."

"Ahhh. You are a sweetheart," said Max, patting Brayden's head.

"I wish you'd fly kites with us," Parker said. "And afterwards, would you take us on a pony ride?"

"It would have to be a stick horse. A real pony would toss you off because you smell so bad," Brayden muttered.

"Not me. I actually use soap," Gavin argued.

"Yeah, you..."Brayden trailed off as Kenzie and some of her friends walked by their table. He caught her eye and smiled. She scowled back at him and kept walking.

"Looks like you made a friend today," said Trey.

The other guys snorted.

Ian smirked. "I'll bet she'd like you if you invited her over to fly kites."

Brayden threw his backpack on the couch after school. He ignored Banjo, who was jumping at his feet, and targeted his mom. "You told Ian's mom that I flew kites with Willow?"

"I suppose. I thought it was sweet."

"Well, so did Ian! He told all of the guys about it at school."

Mom covered her mouth, attempting to hide her smile. "I really didn't mean for news of your kindness to spread."

"Not funny, Mom. See if I ever do that again."

Mom's smile vanished. "Now wait. I am sorry. I really didn't think about your friends finding out. I promise to keep your good moments to myself."

Brayden ignored her and clomped up to his room. A few minutes later he stomped right back down the stairs. "Who left the lid off my cricket jar?"

"Why would anyone touch your cricket jar?" asked his mom. "*I* don't want near those things. I doubt if anyone else does either."

"Oh, yeah? Well, all of Mac's crickets escaped and they couldn't get out on their own. There's no way Mac's gecko arms could unscrew the lid. What do I feed him now? I suppose the crickets are just hanging out in my room some place waiting to hop back in the jar. Right?"

Willow started to slink out of the room.

Brayden blocked her escape route. "Willow, did you let my crickets go?" he demanded.

She froze. "Not on purpose."

"Not on purpose," Brayden mimicked. He smacked his forehead. "What were you doing with them? Why were you even in my room?"

"I just wanted to watch your gecko eat a cricket. I thought I put the lid back on, but I guess I forgot."

"How could you forget? Oh, wait. *I* forgot. You're just a pesky little sister," he shouted. "Now I guess you get to go look for the crickets and see if you can put them back in the jar."

Willow's eyes filled with tears. "I didn't mean to—"

"It doesn't matter. Mac needs food and I don't want crickets hopping around in my room making annoying chirping sounds until they die. Go find them!"

22

Willow looked at her feet. "I'll try," she said in a tiny voice.

Brayden felt some of the rage ooze out when he saw her stricken face. A pang of guilt plucked at his ribcage. He almost said something, but crossed his arms instead.

"That was a bit harsh," said his mom. Disappointment seeped deep into her eyes. "You don't have to worry about me bragging about *that* scene to Ian's mom. I hate crickets, but I think I'll help your sister try to find some of them." She followed Willow up the stairs.

Brayden watched them leave. Regret began to gnaw at his conscience, but it would not feast until much later.

CHAPTER 3

CRISP MORNING AIR

The next morning, the house was filled with the aroma of eggs and bacon sizzling in a skillet. Brayden threw on a shirt and khakis and shuffled to the table, finger-combing his hair on the way. His beagle was already wolfing down Dog Chow, so only wagged his tail to acknowledge family approaching.

"Why does the bacon look different?" Brayden asked.

Each strip of meat was a uniform peach color, lacking the marbled fat and meat design.

"I was hoping you wouldn't notice," admitted Mom. "I thought we'd try turkey bacon this morning."

Dad sighed. "Let me guess. It's healthier?"

Mom nodded.

"Do you really think we need to try something new two days in a row? I really like my normal bacon," Dad said.

Mom grabbed her slightly melted plastic spatula and scooped two pieces of bacon onto his plate. "The doctor told you to take better care of yourself. I don't want you having a heart attack or getting diabetes. Besides, we all could benefit from eating better."

Willow bit into the bacon and shrugged. "Not bad. I don't like the idea of eating cute little pigs anyhow. That's what regular bacon is, right?"

"What about a cute little turkey?" asked Brayden. "You don't mind a feathered friend having to give its life for you to eat a healthy breakfast?"

She frowned and dropped the bacon onto her plate. "I guess I'll just eat my eggs."

"Thanks, Brayden," Mom said.

"No problem. Just keeping it real."

"Keep it real much longer and we'll all be eating vegetarian. That would be even healthier," Mom stated.

Dad clenched his fork. "I'm sure Brayden is done talking. I like my meat."

Brayden sighed. "I just—"

"Not another word," Dad interrupted.

Brayden bristled, his spine stiff. He gnawed at his turkey bacon in silence. They could hear the wind gusting and tormenting their trees again. A limb scraped on the siding.

"Did you ever clip the branches like I asked?"

Brayden looked down at his plate.

"Answer me," Dad commanded.

"You told me not to talk."

"Don't be smart with me. Did you clip the branches?"

"You probably wouldn't be hearing them if I had."

The ticking clock seemed to increase in volume. The wind grew louder as well, spitefully shoving the branches into the house again. Dad's face turned red and it looked like he would explode at any minute.

Willow looked back and forth between Brayden and her Dad and squirmed in her wooden chair. "So...Great weather we're having," she said.

No one responded.

"I was thinking it would be a good day to bike to school," she continued. "That way, Dad wouldn't have to drop us off on his way to work."

Dad turned to her and his color faded. He looked at the clock and washed down his bacon with a swallow of orange juice. "Good idea. I have extra work I need to get done anyhow." He carried his plate to the sink and plucked his keys off the key ring by the door. "Brayden," he said taking a deep breath and closing his eyes, "get the tree limbs cut today right after school. We'll talk about your attitude when I get home."

Mom and Willow gave Dad a hug before he left. Brayden stared at the eggs on his plate.

"I'll go get shoes on so I can bike with both of you," said Mom.

"When are you going to let us bike by ourselves?" asked Brayden. "I'd never hear the end of it if the guys saw you biking with me."

"I'd consider it if Willow's school started before yours. I don't want her to be on her own once you get to school. There are too many crazy people out there looking for kids to grab. I just want to keep her safe. Besides--I need the exercise." She patted her backside and shook her head.

"Then can you both bike a little behind me?" Brayden asked. "This day is already off to a bad start. I don't need humiliation to make it worse." He dumped his eggs into Banjo's food dish and returned his plate to the table. "Where's my backpack?"

"You left it on the living room floor, so I hung it up in the laundry room," Mom stated as she tied her shoes.

Brayden retrieved the backpack and groaned. "Great. It was touching Willow's backpack so now it smells like baby powder and flowers."

"You're welcome," Willow said. "That's much better than your backpack's sweat and body odor."

"That's your opinion. Now the guys will have something else to make fun of."

"Your friends stink."

"So do yours."

"Oh yeah? Mine don't make fun of people for nothing." Willow turned to her mom and put her skinny arms on her hips. "If this is what being a teenager is like, I don't think I want to be one."

All three of them strapped on their helmets as the garage door moaned and squealed open. They pedaled down the driveway, avoiding the cracks that plagued its surface.

Brayden inhaled the crisp morning air until it drowned out the powdery flower smell from his backpack. He picked up speed on his bike until his mom and sister were several car lengths behind him. Sometimes he just needed space. He mulled over the morning. How had a conversation about turkey bacon ended in so much arguing?

He slowed his bike to avoid kids walking to school. It was like they couldn't hear him coming. He needed a horn on his bike so he could warn people to let him through. Some of Willow's friends had little bells or squeaky horns on their bikes. They sounded too girly. He needed to find a horn blast that made people jump and move.

He had to swerve off the sidewalk for three girls talking side by side. He jolted over clumps of grass and rock until he passed them.

"Oh, excuse me," he said with a sarcastic tone.

"You're not excused," one of the girls called after him.

"That was clever," he retorted.

He hit the brakes when he reached the stop light, and punched the crossing button. Willow and Mom caught up to him. Brayden stared straight ahead.

"I think we should get off our bikes right now and hug your brother, don't you?" asked Mom.

"Good idea. Then the whole world will know we're biking together." Willow giggled.

"Very funny," Brayden muttered without turning his head. "You wouldn't dare."

Willow hopped off her bike and propped up her kick stand. "Oh, really?"

The crossing light changed just in time. Brayden pedaled away as fast as he could, shaking his head.

"We love you," Mom called after him. "Have a good day at school, sweetheart."

"Yeah, dear brother," Willow yelled.

Brayden locked his bike to the steel stand beside the school, yanked off his helmet and jammed it on his handle bars. He scanned the other kids walking to the main door. They ignored him. He sighed in relief. No one had witnessed that scene. He adjusted his backpack and walked through the glass door.

The three girls he passed on his bike entered right behind him.

"Maybe you should ride your bike with your mommy and sister the entire way. You might learn some manners," one of the girls said.

Her friends laughed.

"*You* should ride with them. You might learn how to actually be funny," Brayden snapped back.

28

Her expression darkened. She spun on her heel and walked away, her friends right behind her.

Brayden slammed his books into his locker, causing an avalanche with his notebooks and pencils. They spilled out at his feet. Two pencils kept rolling into the middle of the hall. A short kid with a Star Wars t-shirt stepped on a pencil and landed flat on his back. His papers scattered across the hall.

Brayden groaned. "Really? This had to happen today?" He rolled his eyes. "Are you okay?"

The kid gave him a blank look, but tried to sit up. He rubbed his sore back. Brayden grabbed his arm to help him to his feet.

Ian stepped up behind them. "Don't worry about it, Brayden. He's just a freshman. They trip over their own feet. Right, Freshman?"

The kid brushed off his Star Wars shirt and started picking up his papers. He frowned but nodded.

"See? Let's go."

Max herded Brayden down the hall to meet with the rest of their buddies. He started laughing.

"That was classic. You guys should have seen it. Brayden's stuff spills out of his locker, and this freshman totally trips on a pencil. He landed, wham! Flat on the floor." Ian doubled over, laughing.

The other guys joined in, pounding Brayden on the back. Brayden forced a smile. Kenzie and her friend, Marissa, walked by. She glanced at them and shook her head. Brayden scowled. Today just kept getting worse.

He slumped into his chair in World History. Mr. Montoya immediately began his lecture, pacing back and forth in front of the class. Brayden closed his eyes. He couldn't even pretend to be interested today. Minutes passed but they felt like hours. Brayden replayed the breakfast scene with his dad, recalling the command to clip the branches and discuss his attitude. It seemed like he was getting lots of talks about his attitude lately.

"So, Brayden? Did you hear me? I asked everyone to turn in their homework," Mr. Montoya said. "We're waiting on you."

"Oh. Yeah."

He opened up his notebook and flipped to his history section. It was empty. He smacked his head. The assignment must have fallen out of the folder when his locker exploded.

"Did you forget to do it?" asked Mr. Montoya.

"No. I did it," Brayden mumbled. "It just fell out of my notebook this morning."

"Just fell out, did it? Well, I guess you get to do it *again* tonight for ten points off."

"Why not? My day doesn't stink enough already," he mumbled.

"What was that?" Mr. Montoya asked. "Do you need a few more points off for your attitude?"

The rest of the class turned to stare at him.

Brayden stifled a sharp comeback. "No," he finally managed to say.

"Good. I'll expect your assignment tomorrow. You're all dismissed."

Brayden kept his chin high, silently daring any of his classmates to make a comment. He felt like a ticking time bomb as he stalked away.

A girl with much needed braces and a unibrow stood in front of his locker. She backed away the moment she saw the surly expression on his face. He shoved his World History book into his locker and grabbed supplies for his next two classes. He took his time at the drinking fountain, trying to simmer down.

Science was tolerable, but in English, he realized yet another assignment was missing. While his classmates passed their papers forward, Brayden tried explaining his dilemma to Mr. Hankenson, who responded with even less sympathy than Mr. Montoya.

Kenzie leaned over and whispered, "Maybe next time you make someone fall, you'll help him pick up his papers. Chances are, you would have found some of your own."

"If you're so perfect, why didn't *you* help him?" Brayden hissed.

"Actually, I did. But I didn't inspect the papers to see who they belonged to. Daniel--yes the freshman has a name--was in a hurry to get to class so he wouldn't hear all of you laughing."

Brayden's anger swelled by noon, desperate for release. He joined his buddies at their lunch table.

"There he is," Ian said, grinning. "I've had a great morning, thinking about that freshman you made fall. I wish I had a video camera going. That would have gone viral on YouTube."

"Yeah. That was hilarious," Brayden snapped. He dug through his paper sack and grabbed a bag of chips. He tore it open and began to chomp each chip, letting crumbs fall to the table.

Trey jammed half of his pizza slice into his mouth. "Does anyone want to hang out at my place after school? I was going to shoot some hoop."

Max shrugged. "Sure. Why not?"

"I'm in," said Gavin.

"Me, too," Ian said.

Brayden kept eating chips.

"What about you?" asked Trey, grabbing the chip bag.

Brayden grabbed it back. "I can't this time. I have to clip some branches that are hitting my house."

"So do it afterwards," said Max.

"Nah. I got into a fight with my dad and he wants it done right after school." Brayden reached into his bag and pulled out a ham sandwich in a Ziploc bag. It had a hot pink sticky note clinging to the side.

Ian snatched the note. "What's this?" He read it out loud in a nasal tone made easy by his long beak of a nose. "Dad won't be mad long. Have a GRRRRReat day. Love, Willow."

Brayden reached for the note, but Gavin got it first. "Oh, look. There's a *cute* tiger drawing. He must be the one saying GRRRRReat. Isn't that *adorable*?"

The guys started laughing. Brayden grabbed the note and crumpled it up.

"Oh, don't ruin it. That note was *precious*," said Trey.

Ian pounded Brayden on the back. "No wonder you like to fly kites with your sister. She is so *sweet*."

"You guys are hilarious," said Brayden through clenched teeth.

His afternoon included another missing homework page in Spanish, a lecture in Computers for taking out his anger on the keyboard, and more teasing about the pink note in the locker room. Brayden could not get out of the high school building soon enough. He crammed his helmet on his head and unlocked his bike.

Three girls with familiar faces walked by. One stopped and smiled. "Are you waiting for your mommy and sissy to pick you up?"

"Are you waiting for your boyfriend? Oh wait. You don't have one." He looked her over. "I can see why." Brayden got on his bike and pedaled furiously all of the way home.

CHAPTER 4

APRIL SHOWERS

As soon as Brayden walked through the front door, he threw his backpack on the tile floor, grabbed the clippers from the garage and began attacking the maple tree. The buds had transformed into vibrant green leaves, but Brayden was too annoyed to care. Old branches and tender new shoots were all targets for his frustration.

Mom walked up behind him. "Something wrong?"

Brayden continued whacking off branches.

"I'll take that as a yes. Would you like to talk about it?"

"No." He chopped some more.

"Just keep in mind that I actually like that tree and want it to have some branches left when you're done. I'm going to bike to your sister's school to pick her up." She disappeared into the garage.

Brayden stopped cutting and took four steps backwards. The tree was now lopsided and had huge bare spots. There was no way it would scrape the side of the house, but it looked rather pathetic. He hurled the clippers to the ground and started gathering branches. After piling them up, he tied them with twine and dragged them to the end of the driveway. Mom and Willow biked past him.

"Hey, Brayden," said Willow. She struggled with the helmet buckle under her chin. "Did you see my note?"

Brayden's temper flared. "I saw it. And so did all of the guys. Thanks a lot. They teased me about it for the entire lunch break."

Willow wilted. "I thought it would cheer you up. You used to like when mom put notes in your lunch."

"Maybe in first grade. No one does cutesy notes in high school!"

Tears began to well up in her eyes. She pulled off her helmet. Her wispy hair stuck out in every direction. "I was just trying to help. You seemed upset this morning. Most people like my drawings. I wanted to make you smile again."

"You know what would make me smile? If you would leave me alone and stop embarrassing me!"

"Fine!" Willow dropped her helmet and ran into the house.

Brayden stood for a while, breathing heavily. He stooped down to pick up her helmet. A crack now zigzagged down the middle of the purple outer shell. He carried it into the garage and hung it on her bike's handlebars, and then slumped to the cement floor.

The day had been a complete disaster, and he had just taken it all out on his sister. A long-legged spider gradually descended right in front of him. It landed on the cracked helmet and scurried across the smooth surface. Brayden flicked it off. He already dreaded a talk with his dad. Now he needed to talk things over with his sister, too. It was Friday. The weekend would be very long if he couldn't work things out with his family.

He pulled himself to his feet and trudged inside. Mom was rolling out pizza dough. Flour flecked her cheeks. She looked up as Brayden entered the kitchen, but remained silent. Their beagle howled and ran down the stairs to greet him. His tail whacked back and forth as he jumped at Brayden's feet.

"I think you're the only one I didn't upset today."

He bent down and scratched behind Banjo's floppy brown ear. The dog licked his hand.

Brayden continued up the stairs and peeked into Willow's room. She sat on the floor, hunched over her purple notebook. A yellow bulldozer decorated the top of the page and she was writing furiously underneath it. Her letters were not as loopy as usual. They were dark, stiff angry letters.

"Can I talk to you?" asked Brayden.

"No," Willow answered. "You said to leave you alone, so I am. Besides, I'm busy writing another story."

"Can we talk when you aren't mad?"

"We'll see. Close the door behind you," she instructed without even looking up.

Brayden did as she asked and wandered to his own room. He flopped onto his bed and stared up at the ceiling. Friday nights were family nights. Would anyone even want him around? Part of him wanted to just leave. He was tempted to go biking somewhere so he didn't have to face everyone. Better yet, if he would finally get his license, he could drive around.

He sighed. It looked like he would actually have to do some repair work. He grabbed a scrap piece of paper off his desk, scribbled "I'm sorry" on it and stuffed it under Willow's door. No response. It was worth a try. He shuffled downstairs, grabbed his backpack and returned to his room.

He might as well get started on some of his missing assignments.

An hour later, he heard a paper rustling as someone shoved it under his door. He rolled off the bed and grabbed the purple picture. A bumblebee with crossed legs was drawn on top and had a conversation balloon beside it that said, "I forgive you, but BEE nicer or BUZZ off."

Brayden actually smiled. He tossed the note on his desk and grabbed another piece of paper. He scribbled "I'll BEE better BEEhaved" on top and stuffed it under her door.

"Dinner!" Mom called.

The smell of pepperoni and melted mozzarella drifted through the air and lured everyone to the kitchen table. Maybe the awful day was improving. His mouth watered as Mom pulled oven mitts onto her hands and carried a pizza to the table.

Dad pushed open the door while talking on his cell phone. Brayden felt a knot twist in his stomach. His challenging day wasn't completely over. Dad hung up his keys, ended his phone call and joined the rest of his family at the table. Mom prayed and they began helping themselves to pizza slices.

"So, I noticed you clipped the tree," Dad said. "A lot. It certainly won't be scratching the house any time soon."

Brayden hung his head. "I had a tough day at school and took it out on the tree...and on people. I'm over it."

"I hope your disrespect is over, too. If you are learning that attitude from your friends at school, we can arrange for some time away from them. I've seen the guys acting up after football games. I don't mind giving you time apart."

"I'll watch what I say," Brayden promised. He shifted in his chair, anxious to change subjects.

"Good. I'm going to hold you to that." Dad grabbed another slice. "Good pizza. It seems…normal."

Mom sighed. "It *is* normal. I used regular pepperoni. Willow requested it for her family night." She turned to her daughter. "So, what do we get to do this fine evening?"

Willow wiped pizza sauce off her chin. "The Scribble Competition. And the winner gets to decide the next game we play."

"Yea. I wonder who will win this time," said Brayden. "You're always drawing."

"I can't help it. Art is my life," Willow said clutching her heart dramatically.

The family devoured two pizzas and worked together to wash the dishes and wipe down the blue vinyl placemats. Willow hummed an unfamiliar tune as she placed four pieces of white paper and four sharpened pencils on the coffee table. Brayden felt his tension dissolve. He was grateful that he had escaped Dad's dog house. The family gathered around the table, sitting with their legs criss-crossed. Even Dad was on the floor. He had traded his dry clean pants for jeans.

"Everyone scribble," Willow instructed.

Her family drew elaborate scribbles on their papers.

"Now pass the scribbles to the person on your left," she said.

Papers were passed.

"Get ready to turn the scribble into a picture. We have five minutes. Set the stopwatch, please, Daddy."

Dad pulled his black framed reading glasses out of his shirt pocket and slid them on his face. He hit buttons on his watch and gave Willow a thumbs up sign.

"Okay. On your mark, get set, go!"

Brayden, Willow and Mom quickly began to draw. Dad sat deep in thought and then looked at Mom's picture.

"No cheating!" she scolded, covering her picture.

He scratched his graying brown hair and finally began drawing. Five minutes went by before his watch began to beep.

"Pencils down!" Willow commanded. "Everyone examine the pictures."

They bent over the artwork. Mom's drawing was of a birthday cake with forty-two candles on top. The cake looked like it had caught on fire. Brayden had drawn a picture of a peanut butter and jelly sandwich with a seven-legged spider on top.

"Oops," he said, adding the eighth leg.

Dad's picture was a partially completed stick man holding a coffee cup. Willow's drawing centered on a detailed monkey playing a banjo while eating a banana and roller skating, using his tail as a leash for a puppy.

"Time to vote," said Willow. "Raise your hand for the birthday cake."

Only Willow raised her hand.

"How about the sandwich and spider?"

No hands went up.

"The man with the coffee?"

No hands.

"The busy monkey?"

Mom, Dad and Brayden raised their hands.

"Like we had a chance against the resident artist," said Dad. "I guess we know who gets to chose the games."

The rest of the evening was spent playing card games. The winner from each round had to run a victory lap around the living room. Dad ran the most laps and reminded the family of that fact repeatedly as they got ready for bed.

Brayden sniffed the air. Could that be pancakes? If his nose was correct, that would actually be worth getting out of bed. He stumbled to the kitchen, yawned and rubbed his eyes. Dad and Willow already sat at the table, cutting into golden-brown pancakes.

Mom stood in front of the stove with a spatula in her hand. "Any special requests?"

"Nah. Any shape is fine."

"I have a flower," Willow said, cutting off a petal bite and stuffing it into her mouth. "A daisy, to be exact."

"Mine is a..." Dad looked at his pancake in confusion. "Honey, what is mine again?"

Mom scowled. "A fish. I just accidentally dropped some extra batter on his head."

"A circle is fine, Mom," said Brayden.

"Too boring. You get a bike."

"Whatever." Brayden sat at the table.

"Oops. I guess this looks more like a tricycle." Mom flipped a lumpy pancake onto his plate.

Brayden smothered the pancake with syrup and ate it in four bites.

"Can I have another one?" he asked.

"Already? Okay, this time you get a circle after all."

The sky darkened to a pale gray. Mom flipped on the kitchen light and continued cooking. Thunder rumbled outside and rain began to fall, forming puddles on their newly water-proofed deck. Two doves perched on the deck railing side-stepped until they were sheltered by the bird feeder.

Brayden groaned. "I was going to play basketball today."

"After you mowed the lawn," added Dad.

"Yeah. That too."

"When do I get to start mowing the lawn?" asked Willow.

"When you gain fifty pounds and a little muscle," said Brayden. "You're so scrawny the lawnmower would run away with you."

"Would not," Willow protested.

"Have you looked in the mirror lately?" teased Brayden. "You could pass for a first grader."

"That's enough," said Dad.

The rain intensified, splattering against the windows. The grass and trees soaked it in. The April showers had been more abundant this year. Daffodils and tulips were blooming early and the grass was growing long and green.

"I was going to work in my garden," said Mom, pulling her frizzy blond hair into a short pony tail, "but a lazy Saturday reading a book sounds good, too."

Later that afternoon, Brayden walked past Willow's room. She was sitting on a checkered blanket on her floor. A stuffed dog, two teddy bears and a sock monkey were all propped up around the blanket with tea cups at their feet. Willow poured water from a fancy floral tea pot into each of their cups.

"Care to join us?" she asked.

"Nope. I'm not a tea party sort of guy."

"You used to be."

"Maybe when I was two."

"Come on. None of your buddies will ever know."

"Yeah. I thought that about flying kites, and somehow that leaked out."

"Are you sure? The tea is delicious."

"I'll pass. I can have luke-warm water any time."

"Fine. Mom!" she hollered. "Can you join my tea party?"

Mom ventured in and smiled. She sat beside the teddy bear that was wearing a straw hat. "I'd love to. Tea, please."

Willow poured tea into her cup. They clinked their cups together and each took a sip with their pinky fingers extended.

Brayden shook his head and returned to his room. He would much rather attempt to defeat zombies on an electronic device. If he could have seen into the future, he might have reconsidered the tea party offer.

CHAPTER 5

PELTING RAIN

Stormy weather forced Mom to drive Brayden and Willow to school for several days. The wind pestered the rain drops, blowing them diagonally, making it too difficult for anyone to ride a bike. On Wednesday morning, the rain finally decreased to a mild drizzle. Willow insisted on walking to school so she could wear her new spotted mud boots and purple jacket. She popped open the over-sized striped umbrella and huddled underneath it with Mom.

Brayden refused to use an umbrella, and he grumbled the entire walk to school. Mom and Willow did not have to listen, as they were asked to walk a considerable distance behind him so he wouldn't be embarrassed.

By the time he entered the front doors of high school, Brayden's hair, shorts and shoes were soaked. He shook off his jacket and jammed it into his locker.

"What's with the drowned rat look?" asked Max. "You couldn't get a ride? You'd better get your license soon."

"My sister wanted to walk," Brayden muttered.

"Did you all skip and hold hands on the way?" asked Ian.

"Funny."

"So did you get my text last night?" asked Trey.

Brayden shook his head.

"Oh, man. You've got to look," Ian said, snickering. "Logan's going to freak when he sees it."

Brayden flipped on his phone and searched his messages. He opened Trey's text. It showed a picture of Logan in the locker room without his t-shirt. He was rubbing his skinny bicep. The text read, "Grow, muscle, grow. I don't want girl arms forever."

The guys huddled around the phone and laughed so hard they were doubled over. Brayden didn't find it that funny, but chuckled anyhow.

Walking to class was a breeze. Some students stood in clumps by their lockers, passing phones around. Most of them were laughing. Everyone remaining in the hall cleared a wide path for Brayden and his friends.

"Good one, Trey," someone called out.

"Who else got that text?" asked Brayden.

"Everyone I know. They probably forwarded to everyone they know. Logan will be famous."

Brayden shoved the text out of his mind during World History and Science. He sat by Trey and Max during English and looked at the assignment board. His stomach churned when he realized he hadn't completed his essay. He dug through his notebook and began writing furiously.

Max whistled. Trey joined in, accompanied by several other students in class. Brayden looked up from his paper in confusion. Logan was walking toward his seat. His face was bright red and he slumped into his chair.

"Can I see your girl arms?" asked a boy Brayden didn't even know.

Kenzie scowled. "Leave him alone!"

"Or what?"

"Logan needs a girl to protect his girl arms," said Max.

Logan hid his face with his notebook. Several classmates laughed and whistled again.

Mr. Hankenson entered the room carrying a steaming cup of coffee. "Do we have a problem here?"

"No, sir," Max answered.

"Then what's the commotion?" Mr. Hankenson scanned the room. "Logan? Are you okay?"

Logan looked up and nodded.

"Then let's get to work. Everyone pull out your essays. We'll take turns reading them out loud."

Brayden wrote even faster, stopping only when the teacher looked his way. He finished right before his name was called. The essay was certainly not his best work, but at least it was done. Every time he paused during his reading, his eyes seemed to stray to Kenzie. She glared back at him.

"Your turn, Trey," said Mr. Hankenson.

"I'll have to read it tomorrow," Trey said. "I was too busy to finish it last night."

The rest of the class snickered, with the exception of Logan, Kenzie and a few of her friends.

"That will cost you twenty points."

"Got it."

"Logan. Your turn."

"I'll pass for today," Logan said.

Mr. Hankenson choked on his coffee. "You what?"

"I will read my essay another time."

"But you have a perfect score in this class. You heard me tell Trey that waiting will cost him twenty points, right?"

"Yes, sir."

"Are you sick?"

"I've felt better."

"Maybe you should go to the nurse. I'll write you a pass."

Logan slunk up to the front and grabbed the pass just as the bell rang. He stuffed it in his pocket and waited behind the desk until the class finished pouring out of the room. His shoulders were stooped over as he rushed to the nurse's office. Kenzie started to follow him, but turned to pursue Brayden and his friends instead.

"I know one of you sent the text about Logan," she said from behind them.

Trey spun around. "Did you get the text?"

"No. And I'm glad."

"Then how can you prove who sent it?" Max asked.

"I can ask around."

"And then what?" Ian joined in. "Everyone knows that snitches become the next target. Is that what you want?"

Kenzie didn't answer.

"I didn't think so," Ian said with a smirk. "So maybe you should mind your own business from now on."

The guys turned and left Kenzie isolated in the hall. Brayden looked back at her with an apologetic grin.

She rolled her eyes at him. "Self-absorbed bullies," she muttered. Revulsion dripped from her words. She stomped off in the opposite direction.

Brayden took his time at his locker. He was not looking forward to another class with Kenzie. She was a fire ready to combust and evidently he and his friends were matches. He finally wandered into Algebra II just before the tardy bell, and was surprised to see the principal standing at the door. Had Kenzie or someone else told him about the text? Was he here to round up all of Trey's friends for questioning? Would they be expelled?

Brayden avoided eye contact as he walked past the large man with a goatee and slid into his chair. He tried to look like a responsible student as he pulled out his homework and pretended to study the next page in his textbook.

"You all probably have an idea why I am here," the principal began.

Brayden slipped further down into his chair. Here it came. His dad would definitely make him hang out with different guys after this.

"Mrs. Brinkhaus had to leave suddenly to pick up her sick child. No substitutes were available, so I will fill in for her remaining class sessions today. Go ahead and pass your homework forward. Then you may begin on the assignment she wrote on the board."

Brayden exhaled. He began his homework immediately, grateful for the first time all year that he was staying in math class. He actually finished all of his assignment by the time the bell rang.

The guys were at their lunch table, pointing at the office. Logan was checking out of school for the day. He pulled his tan jacket over his head as he hustled toward the front entrance.

Trey whistled. All of the other guys at the table joined in. Max nudged Brayden's arm when he noticed he was just sitting. Brayden whistled too.

"Did you see how Logan covered his head walking past us? Do you think it was to shield his face from our glow of greatness, or did he think it was raining inside?" asked Max.

The early morning drizzle intensified by the time school was out for the day, and the wind was shifting from mischievous to spiteful. Brayden was relieved to see a text from his mom telling him to meet her in the parking lot. Willow must have decided that even *she* didn't want to walk in this much rain and wind. His mom flashed the headlights of their black Toyota Camry as he approached. Mom's oversized brown purse oozed its contents into the front passenger seat, so he lunged into the back seat, slamming the door quickly behind him. He shook out his hair like their beagle, splattering the vinyl head rest in front of him.

"We have some errands to run," Mom said. "I hope you don't mind getting a ride today. I know how much you enjoy walking in the rain."

"I think I'll survive. Where are we going?"

"We have to go to Meyer's Music Store. Willow needs a new reed for her clarinet—"

"My band teacher says chipped reeds make clarinets sound like sick ducks."

"—and I figured while we were on that side of town we could finally check out that new Sporting Goods store you've been asking about."

Brayden smiled. "Oh, yeah. I'd about given up on that idea."

"Sorry. I just don't drive out that far if I can help it." She turned the windshield wipers up a notch. "I wouldn't be going there in this nasty weather if it wasn't for Willow's reed emergency."

"I've got to sound good for my band test tomorrow. I want to be first chair for our final concert," Willow said. She leaned forward in her seat. "Dad got that night off from work, right?"

"Of course. We'll all be there."

Brayden groaned.

"We'll ALL be there, and we'll ALL love it," Mom said.

"Can I bring ear buds and listen to some *real* music?" asked Brayden.

Willow punched his arm.

"Mom! Willow hit me. Or at least I *think* she hit me. Her scrawny arms couldn't hurt a flea."

"That's because your arm has so much padding. You need to lay off the chips, bud." Willow puffed out her cheeks.

"It's called muscle. You wouldn't know because you've never had any."

"I'm petite—and glad about it."

"That's almost the right word. How about *pipsqueak*?"

"Enough, you two," Mom said. "Willow has sat through all of your football games without bringing her own entertainment. You'll do the same for her."

"Yeah. And most of the time, you aren't even playing. You're just sitting on the bench, yelling," Willow teased.

"Not next year. Coach always gives juniors more playing time," Brayden insisted.

"If that happens, I'll make up some embarrassing cheers to do in the stands." She waved her arms, holding imaginary pompoms. "Brayden's got the ball. Now he's going to fall. I want to shop at the mall...Yea, team!" She giggled.

"For being a good writer, that cheer kind of stunk," Brayden said.

"Wow. You called me a good writer. You must be tired if you're handing out compliments."

"I am. Now stop talking so I can take a nap. It's been a long day." He leaned against the car window and closed his eyes.

Willow began humming a lullaby in an overly sweet voice. Brayden shook his head and plugged his ears until her song finally ended.

"Wake up!"

Two light blue eyes were inches from his own. Brayden jerked back with a start. Willow's musical peals of laughter brought him to his senses.

"We're here," Mom said. "It's pouring so we're going to run in at the same time. Ready?"

Brayden rubbed his eyes and pulled his black jacket over his head. Mom and Willow zipped their jackets and flipped up their hoods.

"Go!"

The three of them jumped out of the car and raced through the pelting rain. By the time they dived inside Meyer's Music, their jackets, shorts, and shoes were soaked.

"Nice weather, isn't it?" asked the sales clerk. He waited until they lowered their hoods. "What can I help you find?"

"We need a reed for my clarinet," Willow stated.

"Right this way."

They passed shelves with replacement guitar strings and picks, fluffy pad savers and cleaning rods. The clerk skipped the reed display for saxophones, oboes and bassoons, and showed them brand options specifically for the clarinet. Willow selected the reed her band director preferred and they returned to the cash register. The clerk scanned the reed and informed them of the cost.

The tornado siren suddenly began to wail. Willow jumped, bumping into a sheet music display. Popular songs from the last decade fluttered to the floor. She quickly began to pick up the fallen music.

"Relax, Willow," said Brayden, leaning against the counter. "This is Wednesday. And it's May 1st. They always test the tornado siren on the first Wednesday of the month."

He watched her stuff music back in the display without offering assistance.

Mom walked to the glass store front window. "Usually they test them in the morning, but you could be right."

"I'll check the radio and make some calls," said the clerk. "You're welcome to stay here until the siren stops or the storm passes."

"Isn't the Sporting Goods store just two doors down?" asked Brayden. "I'd rather wait there. At least we can look around. We wouldn't even get wet because the sidewalk connecting both stores is covered by the roof overhang."

"I'd rather stay here," said Willow.

"But we already got what you needed," Brayden argued. "We could be to the other store in five seconds."

Mom turned to the clerk. "Any news yet?"

He held the phone up to his ear, but shook his head. "I'm calling the manager to see what he wants us to do. He's checking weather reports."

The siren faded for a moment.

"There. That's probably it. Can we go?" Brayden asked.

Mom looked outside again. The rain continued to pour, but the wind appeared better behaved, merely swaying branches and randomly plucking off wet leaves. "Okay. Quick."

They all ran down two doors to the Sporting Goods store. The door was locked. They searched for the sign posting the hours.

"It shouldn't close until 7:00," said Brayden. He looked at his watch. "It's only 4:32."

Willow and Brayden pressed their faces to the glass door. The lights were turned off, so only the displays of soccer shoes and baseball gloves were visible near the front.

The siren started up again.

"Really?!" Mom exclaimed. "Back to the music store."

They ran back and pulled on the door. Locked! They peeked through the glass window. The clerk wasn't at the desk.

"Maybe he is already in the back room to wait out the storm," Mom said. She knocked on the door. No answer.

They tried three other doors in the strip mall. All of them were locked, with no one to be seen. The sky was quickly turning an eerie shade of greenish-gray. The wind's deception became clear when it snapped the branch off a nearby pear tree.

Willow's jaw dropped. "This is no drill! What are we going to do?"

"Everyone to the car," Mom said, her voice tight. "We can't just stand on the sidewalk. We're going home."

CHAPTER 6

TORNADO WARNING

The cantankerous wind increased suddenly, snatching at their clothes and bombarding them with stinging rain as they ran to the car. Willow tried to close the door, but stubborn gusts fought her. Brayden climbed over her and slammed it shut. Mom threw the car into reverse and sped out of the parking lot.

"Are you buckled?" she asked, looking over her shoulder.

"Yes," they both answered.

She accelerated onto the main road and flipped on the radio, turning it full volume so they could hear it over the pounding rain.

"...exercise caution. We have a tornado warning in northeast Johnson County until 7:00. I repeat, the storm has been upgraded to a tornado warning because we are seeing an intense core at 90 mph. We are also seeing storm debris. Go to your protected areas. Find basements or interior walls on the lowest level. This is not the time to be on the roads. We'll continue to track it live...stay tuned to—"

Mom turned the radio down and drove faster.

"It said to get off the roads," said Willow.

"I know," Mom answered. "But there's no place to go. Everything is probably closed. It said northeast. We're going south. We should be okay."

"Check out the sky," Brayden said with his face pressed to the window. "The clouds are huddling together down low. It looks cool."

"This is not cool. It's scary!" said Willow. Her voice was rising in pitch.

"Scary, but exciting," said Brayden. "The guys are going to freak out when I tell them we were caught outside in this. What a rush! It's like we're storm chasers."

"Do storm chasers ever die?" asked Willow.

"Probably." Brayden continued to search the sky. "I wish I could record this."

Willow's chin trembled. "I want to get home."

"I'm going as fast as I can," Mom stated. "You're not helping us keep calm, Brayden." She turned the radio back up.

"...are up to 200 miles per hour! A wall cloud has formed and we have rotation—"

Willow started to cry. Mom turned off the radio.

"We're supposed to go into a ditch if it catches up with us," said Brayden.

"There aren't any ditches around here," said Mom, smacking the steering wheel. "There isn't much of anything but cornfields."

Hail started to pelt the car. Brayden covered his ears, but it still sounded like they were in a movie featuring a gun fight. His excitement began morphing into fear.

"It's getting dark, Mommy!" Willow wailed.

"I know, sweetie. Hold on to each other back there. We'll make it."

A tree branch struck the windshield, cracking the glass on the passenger side. Willow screamed. A car fender whirled behind them and struck the hood. Brayden and Mom joined in on the screaming. Brayden tensed, feeling trapped. He spun around in the back seat with Willow squeezing his arm. He squinted, trying to see through the debris.

A cone shape began to creep out of the low-hanging clouds, gradually dipping closer to the ground. Brayden froze for a moment, watching the whirling finger descend.

"No way," he said. "I actually see the funnel." His eyes widened and panic surged through his body. "Mom! It's almost to the ground! Go! Go! Go!"

Mom floored the car, driving through a red light and swerving around a truck and SUV. They stared in horror as the now malicious wind ripped the bike rack from the SUV's bumper and flung it into the air.

"Look out!" Willow yelled.

Mom swerved, narrowly missing the twisted metal. Willow clung to Brayden, closing her eyes. The sound of pounding rain and hail was overpowered by a heavy rumbling noise. It grew louder and louder until it sounded like a freight train was barreling down on them. The car began to shake.

"Oh, please God, no!" Mom exclaimed.

The car windows shattered. Brayden instinctively covered his face, feeling sharp pricks as his hands and arms were cut with glass splinters. He peered under his arms and saw Willow curled into a ball. Blood peppered his arms. He felt an intense suction. His ears popped and he was afraid his head was going to explode. The car started to lift off the ground. Mom dived into the back of the vehicle, trying to cover her kids with her body. The comfort of her arms could not overpower the overwhelming fear growing inside them all.

Suddenly, silence enveloped them. A strong, gassy odor instigated coughing fits from all of them. Brayden peeked around his mom's arms and stared transfixed at the heart of the funnel. A circular opening at least 80 feet wide extended up for half a mile. Whenever lightning flashed, he could see the spinning cloud walls of the tornado. At the lower rim he saw mini-tornadoes whipping like tails as they writhed around, hissing. The noise grew into a piercing shriek and the freight train was suddenly back upon them. The car spun and they slammed to its sides. It began to sound like thousands of nails were being wrenched from boards. He looked up. The top of their car was gone.

Brayden clawed at the car door as the tornado sucked them upwards out of the vehicle. Willow desperately held on to her seat belt. It snapped. Her mouth formed a scream, but it was too hard to hear. He grabbed her legs. She looked down and smiled at him with gratitude. Her purple t-shirt with "Shine On" written in silver glittered letters whipped back and forth. Mom grabbed their arms, but the car kept spinning and she was tossed backwards.

"Mom!" he yelled, but he couldn't even hear himself.

Willow's legs were slipping through his arms. He grabbed her ankles, squeezing as hard as he could. Willow reached for him, her blue eyes wide with terror.

And then she was gone.

"Willow!" Brayden screamed.

A car door hurled toward him, striking him in the head. Everything went black.

Distant sirens made Brayden's head throb. He tried to open his eyes and groaned. Were the tornado sirens still blaring? Was the tornado still on the ground? A light rain forced him to keep blinking. He wiped water off his face, but was shocked to see the water was red. Red rain? No. He wasn't thinking clearly. Rain dripped between his raised fingers, washing them clean. Cuts on his arms trickled blood, but they were repeatedly washed away. Why did his head hurt so much? He touched it again and sucked in his breath. The pain! He pulled his hand away. It was covered in blood. His headache was so intense he could not concentrate. How could he stop the bleeding? He looked down and immediately fell back in pain. His shirt was in tatters. He ripped it off the rest of the way and held it up in the rain to rinse it off. Clenching his teeth, he rolled up the shirt and tied it around the gash on his forehead.

He tried to sit up and clutched his bandaged head. His headache was overwhelming. The sirens weren't helping. He squinted in the rain. Flashing red, blue and yellow lights blinked in the distance. Emergency vehicles. Maybe the tornado was gone. He looked around, bewildered. The car was gone. Mom and Willow were gone!

"Mom!" he shouted. "Willow!"

No answer.

He began breathing hard as panic engulfed him.

"Hold it together," he said out loud. "You'll find them."

He forced himself to his feet, but swayed unsteadily and dropped to his knees. Determination helped him stand again. His vision began to darken. He closed his eyes and held his head until he could see.

A cornfield surrounded him. Or what was left of a cornfield. It looked like a gigantic lawn mower had chewed it up and spit out the remains. The stalks that remained stood motionless. The cruel wind's anger had dissipated, and it chose to flee the scene of its latest tantrum. A huge maple tree was splintered beside him with its roots exposed for all to see. Several trees remained upright, but they belonged in a Halloween scene. Their branches were stripped bare and splintered. Brayden's jaw dropped. The truck they passed on the road was warped and hung precariously in a tree's branches. He stepped closer. The door on the driver side dangled open and creaked in the breeze. No one was inside.

"Willow! Mom!" he called again.

He staggered to the road, holding his head as he fought dizzy spells. Power lines were down and crackling. A stop light was smashed to the ground, but still blinked red. He walked in a wide arc to avoid stepping on it. The remains of a McDonalds M were impaled into a road sign listing street exits. Where were the people? Where was his family? Emergency vehicle sirens still blared. He walked toward the sound and blinking lights.

Further up the road, he saw an overturned car. He hobbled toward it.

"Anyone there?" he asked. "Do you need help?"

He looked into the shattered windshield and toppled backwards. A middle-aged man in a dress shirt and tie was still buckled into the driver's seat. He wasn't moving.

"Hello? Are you okay?" Brayden gritted his teeth and tapped the man's shoulder. He bit his lip and felt for a pulse on his wrist and listened for breathing. Nothing.

Brayden's stomach clenched and he spun around to vomit. He stumbled away. This couldn't be happening.

"Mom! Willow! Answer me!" This nightmare was overwhelming.

He climbed over random tree branches and looked underneath chunks of drywall. How far could the tornado have carried them? Another car rested precariously on its side. Brayden was afraid to look in the broken window, but a baby began to cry. He hurried to the sound.

A young lady with black tangled hair was inside the car, trying to free her baby's car seat from the wreckage. She had a gash on her left arm but no other obvious injuries.

"Can I help?" Brayden asked.

The lady's face snapped toward him in surprise. "Yes. Oh, yes. If you can pull the car seat toward you while I loosen the straps, I might be able to pull my baby out. The buckles are crushed."

Brayden nodded and pulled hard. The baby cried and struggled to move his pinned arms. The mom frantically yanked on the straps until one broke free. She gently slipped the baby out of the seat and cradled him in her arms.

"Thank you so much," she said. Tears ran down her face, mixing with the light rain. "He seems fine. I don't know how, but he doesn't look hurt." She looked at Brayden. "Are *you* going to be okay?"

Brayden felt light-headed, but nodded. "I just hope my mom and sister made it. I can't find them."

"I'll help you look," she said as she swayed with her baby. His cries softened. "I'm Jen, by the way."

"Brayden. Thanks for helping me."

They both looked into vacant cars and under wood fragments. Brayden even lifted part of a roof. The rain finally stopped, making it easier to see further away. He scanned the road and his heart beat faster. Was that their car?

He lurched forward, hope returning. Maybe. Just maybe.

The black Camry looked like someone had used a can opener to pry off the top. The back door was missing and the front end was crumpled. The entire vehicle was battered to a pulp.

"Mom! Willow! Are you here?"

Nothing.

He looked in the back seat. It was empty. The front door on the driver's side was wedged shut, so he ran around to the other side. The door was open and his mom was sprawled on the ground beside the car. Her leg was wedged under the front seat at an odd angle.

"Mom!" he cried.

She did not answer. Her eyes were closed and blood splattered her arms. His heart sank. He knelt beside her, afraid to take her pulse.

"Don't be dead. Don't be dead," he repeated over and over. Tears dripped down his cheeks.

He felt her wrist. Nothing. He moved his fingers, wishing he had paid more attention to his first aid class. His hand started shaking, but it felt like something fluttered. He leaned closer until his ear pressed close to her mouth. He held his own breath until he heard faint, shallow breathing.

"Mom!"

He patted her cheek. What little make-up she wore was smeared and partially washed away.

"Wake up, Mom!" he pleaded.

Her eyes fluttered. She moaned.

"Mom. Mom! I'm here."

She winced in pain, but opened her eyes. "Brayden. Are you okay?" she whispered.

"Yeah. You will be too."

She reached up and touched the turban wrapped around his head. "You're hurt. Is it bad?"

"I don't think so."

"Where's Willow?" she asked.

Brayden swallowed. "I don't know. I've been looking for her, but don't know where she is."

Tears welled up in Mom's eyes.

"Don't worry. I'll find her."

He heard whimpering and turned around. Jen was walking toward them with her baby slung over her shoulder.

"Oh, good," she exclaimed. "You found them. Are they okay?"

"I found my mom. Her leg is pinned, but she's alive. I still haven't found my sister."

Her smile faded. "Don't give up. I found my cell phone about twenty feet from my car. I called for help. An ambulance should be here soon."

"Thanks," Brayden said. "Did you hear that, Mom? Help is on the way."

She tried to smile. "Good. Maybe they can help us find Willow."

Her eyes fluttered shut.

"Stay with me, Mom. I hear the sirens coming closer. Mom? Mom!"

CHAPTER 7

EYE OF THE TORNADO

Brayden stumbled out of the way for the emergency workers. "I think she stopped breathing," he said, grabbing the arm of a man in a dark blue uniform. "Help her!"

The medic pried Brayden's fingers off his arm and searched for Mrs. Kesler's pulse. "I need oxygen and a splint along with that stretcher." He bent down and began performing CPR.

Another man joined him. He tried to free her from the car. "Her leg is wedged under the seat and is broken in at least two places. I'll need bolt cutters to get her out."

Brayden couldn't watch. He staggered toward the ambulance. A doctor was inspecting the baby. Jen sat beside her infant with an anxious look on her face. Her arm was now bandaged with white gauze.

"Miraculously, your son seems fine, but let's still bring him in for observation." The doctor stood. Her eyebrows shot up when she spotted Brayden. "Wait a minute, young man. Let's look at that head wound. Have a seat."

Brayden settled in the doorway of the ambulance as she unwrapped his shirt turban.

She whistled. "You are one tough customer. That's quite the gash there. We need to stitch you up." She held a light to his eyes. "And you have a concussion. Come on in and rest on the stretcher."

"What about my mom?" he asked.

"The guys will take care of her. She's in good hands. Now, go lie down."

Brayden didn't budge. "Wait! My sister's still out there. We have to find her! We have to find Willow!"

"*You* won't be going anywhere. I'll call for help. Describe her to me."

"She's eleven. She's short and skinny and has long, blond hair and blue eyes. I tried to hold on to her. I had her by the ankles...I had her...Our car was sucked into the tornado. The top of the car tore off like it was paper. Willow was being pulled into the air. I held on...then something hit my head..."

"It's okay. I'll call it in. We've got another hour or two of daylight. They'll find her. Try to lie down."

He swallowed hard and slumped down onto the stretcher. She washed his forehead, causing it to sting even more. He bit his lip to keep from shouting.

"Hang in there. I know it hurts. I'll numb you up now."

She dabbed a medicated cotton square on his forehead. He sighed as the pain eased.

"Better, right? Now you might want to close your eyes. I need to give you a shot."

He clenched his eyes shut and felt a burning prick beside his cut. A strange warm feeling crept over his face and it started to go numb. His hand wandered up toward the cut, but the doctor pushed it back down.

"We don't want to have to clean you up again," she said. "Your hands are filthy. Of course, how could they not be, with all you've been through. Now you just keep your eyes closed and I'm going to sew you back together. Don't worry. You won't feel a thing."

Brayden continued to squeeze his eyes shut. He tensed when he felt a tugging sensation as she pulled the thread in and out. Jen reached over and held his hand. He tried to relax by concentrating on the baby's gurgling sounds.

The doctor finally patted his arm. "Okay, young man. Forty-seven stitches later and you're back in one piece. Let's scoot you to the side before we bandage you. It looks like they got your mom free from the wreckage and are going to wheel her in."

"Is she okay?" Brayden asked.

"I'll bet she will be." She wheeled his stretcher over and wrapped his head with bandages.

"One, two, three, lift," a man said.

Brayden sat up. He closed his eyes until the head rush passed. An oxygen mask was strapped to his mom's face and her leg was set and wrapped. Two men wheeled her in place and inserted an IV line into her arm.

"How is she?" Brayden asked.

"We'll know soon. Jen, I need you buckled in. It will be a tight fit, but all of our ambulances are in use right now. Let's go!"

A paramedic slammed the back door shut and started the sirens. Soon they were speeding to the hospital. Brayden tried to keep his eyes focused on his mom, but he felt himself drifting.

Brayden rolled over and felt a tug on his arm.

"Hold on a minute, son. You're hooked up to an IV."

Brayden opened his eyes. "Dad?"

His dad scooted his chair closer to the bed. His reading glasses could not hide his stress and fatigue. "Right here. How are you feeling?"

"My head hurts." He touched the bandages and groaned.

"I would think so. The nurse said you have forty-seven stitches. Not to mention a serious concussion."

"How's Mom?"

"The doctor said she will be fine. Her leg was broken in two places, but they were clean breaks. She came out of surgery a few minutes ago. They just wheeled her into the recovery room. We can visit her once her drugs wear off."

"Good. What about Willow?"

Dad paled and dropped his head into his hands. "They still haven't found her."

"What? Then why aren't you out looking for her? You don't need to waste time sitting by me. Go find her!"

"I *was* looking for her. As soon as they called me, I joined the search. I called everyone I could think of to help me. The police even went out with rescue dogs. They finally had to stop for the night. It's too dark."

"Then they should use flashlights! She could be hurt and cold and wet..."

"They used flashlights for a while, but it wasn't enough and people needed to get home. We'll look more in the morning."

Brayden punched the hospital bed. "I had her. I held onto her legs, but she was being pulled so hard. If I could have held on a little longer...maybe she would have landed beside me."

Dad leaned closer. "You did all you could. No one could have held on to her during a tornado. It's a miracle that you and your mom survived. All three of you could have died today."

"So you think Willow died?" Brayden asked. His eyes were wet and his emotion spilled into every word.

"I hope not, son. We'll know more in the morning."

A nurse shuffled into the room. "Oh, good. You're awake. Let's have a look at you." She checked his pulse and looked into his eyes with a small light. "We'll still need to keep you overnight, but you're improving. Your mom is waking up. Both of you are welcome to visit her. You can wheel the IV along with you."

Dad helped Brayden out of bed and wrapped his arm around his shoulders for support. They walked slowly into the recovery room. Mom's leg was enclosed in a cast. She had a black eye and cuts on her arms, but she was awake. "Hey guys," she croaked.

Dad and Brayden hugged her gently.

"How are you feeling?" Dad asked.

"Like I got tossed around in a tornado," she answered. "Can you prop me up so I can see you better?"

Dad stacked two pillows and helped her lean against them. He handed her the glass of water from her side table. She took a long sip.

"Brayden. Sit down." She patted the bed beside her. "The nurse said she had to sew you up and that you had a concussion. How are you feeling now?"

"Like I got tossed around in a tornado, too." He tried to smile.

She stroked his face. "No one would tell me about Willow. I'm guessing that means there isn't good news."

Dad held her hand. "We searched until dark. We'll try again first thing in the morning."

Mom nodded and closed her eyes, trying to hold in the tears. "I can't believe I tried to outrun the tornado. I didn't know what else to do. Every place was locked down, and there weren't any ditches. It all happened so fast...I'm so sorry..."

"There wasn't anything more you could do. At least you and Brayden survived. And maybe Willow did, too. There's still hope."

Mom nodded and tried to stifle a yawn.

"The medication is probably making you sleepy," Dad said, stroking her rumpled blond hair. "You should rest. I'll walk Brayden back to his room."

She fell asleep before they reached the door. Brayden leaned on his dad as they walked down the hall, pushing his IV stand. He crawled back under the sheet and rested his head on the sterile white pillow.

"Hey, Dad?" he asked.

"Yeah."

"Have you been home since the tornado struck?"

"No."

"You might need to let Banjo out, or you could have a puddle waiting for you."

Dad gave a half-hearted smile. "I'll do that. See you in the morning."

"Right. And we'll go looking for Willow."

Dad cleared his throat. "Right."

Brayden watched his dad leave. He closed his eyes and hoped for sleep, but it eluded him. His head was throbbing like it contained a trapped coal miner, trying to hammer his way through piles of rock. His mind would not shut down. He turned to his side in his sleeping position. The pillow rubbed on his bandages. He rolled to his back and stared at the floral painting on the hospital wall. How could he sleep knowing that Willow was still lost?

He pictured Willow slipping from his hands. Was she alive?

More images flooded through his mind. The funnel touching down and chasing them. Looking over Mom's shoulder into the eye of the tornado. Jen and her baby stuck in the car. The dead man behind his steering wheel. Mom with her leg stuck and bent wrong. The car in the tree. And Willow again. Her blue eyes wide in terror. He shook his head trying to erase the image, but it only made his head ache more.

A pleasantly plump nurse with dark skin walked in with his chart. "How are you doing?" She asked as she started to check his vital signs.

"I can't sleep and my head is throbbing."

"Not surprising. I'll give you a pain-killer. It should help you sleep, too."

"Good. I've got to rest up so I can look for my sister in the morning."

The nurse paused and looked him in the eye. Her voice thickened with compassion. "I heard your story, and I'm so sorry they haven't found your sister yet. I've heard lots of heart-breaking stories today. That tornado filled our hospital with some mighty hurt people. I'm just glad it didn't tear up our hospital, too. So many people need a place to heal."

"Yeah," Brayden said. His eyelids were growing heavy.

The little nurse stood by his bed. "That's it. Rest easy. And may God be with you for whatever you have to face tomorrow."

CHAPTER 8

MUDDY SHOES

Sunlight poured through the hospital window and warmed Brayden's face and arms. He stretched and realized he was still hooked up to an IV line. His hand drifted to his bandaged head, forcing the events of the last day to flood over him. His stomach churned. If only yesterday had been a nightmare.

A sense of urgency forced his legs out of bed. Willow was still outside somewhere. He stood up quickly. Too quickly. The room grew dark and he had to lean against the wall until his vision cleared. He felt a draft and realized that only a hospital gown covered his boxer shorts. Where were his clothes?

He scanned the room. There was a half-empty glass of water on the night stand. Yes, at a time like this, it was half-empty, not half-full. A padded navy armchair huddled in the corner with a Sports Illustrated magazine tossed on the seat. The bathroom door was cracked open. Brayden lurched over to it. Sink, toilet...and a plastic bag. Brayden grabbed it and looked inside. His muddy shoes were there, but no clothes.

He shuffled back to the bed. Shoes would have to be enough. He was jamming them on his feet when the door opened.

Dad walked in carrying another plastic bag. "How are you?" he asked. "And what are you doing?"

"We've got to start looking for Willow."

"So you were going to search for her in your hospital gown?"

"If I had to. At least I found my shoes."

Dad sighed. "I meant to bring those home last night. Take them off. I have a dry pair for you to wear. And here are some clothes. I don't suppose I can talk you out of helping with the search, right?"

"Right."

"That's what I figured. I'll go check on your mom while you change."

The moment the door closed, Brayden tossed his muddy shoes back into the bag and pulled on faded jeans with the knees blown out. He tried to slip his shirt on over the IV line, but it got caught on his sleeve. Impatiently, he yanked the plastic tube out of his arm and finished dressing.

The same nurse from the previous night knocked on the door and entered. She eyed the IV line. "I figured you'd be anxious to look for your sister. The doctor would prefer you stayed a little longer, but I explained the situation and he signed your release forms. Arm, please."

She cleaned and bandaged where the IV had been inserted, and turned off the drip line. Dad returned and bagged up Brayden's clothes.

"I will be praying for all of you," said the little nurse as they left.

After driving for about five minutes, Dad began to slow down. They were reaching the tornado's path of destruction.

Power lines were still down, but branches and cars had been cleared to the sides of the street.

"The search team said they were going to start where the ambulance found you and your mom. They should already be there. We all looked here once already, but it will be easier with the sun out."

Brayden nodded. They pulled up to their other totaled black Camry. It was now flipped on its side.

A police officer walked up to them and shook their hands. "We just finished rolling the car over, making sure Willow wasn't beneath it. Some firemen also searched the immediate area again...but nothing. We're going to broaden our search now if you want to join us."

"Have you checked the cornfield yet?" asked Brayden. "That's where I was when I woke up."

The police officer cocked his head. "You didn't land near your mom and the car?"

Brayden shook his head. "It took me a while to even find my mom."

"Wait here. I'll round everyone up and we'll follow you."

Minutes later, five police officers with two trained German Shepherds, three fire fighters, and twelve volunteers began to follow Brayden as he tried to remember his path from the night before. The dogs sniffed under Jen's car and the fire fighters double-checked the car that once held the man in the suit. Brayden was grateful that the body had already been removed. He wondered if the family had been notified about their loss.

The group paused by the destroyed McDonald's sign. Brayden pointed up to the truck in the tree.

"I was just beyond this tree."

"That's a memorable landmark," Dad said, craning his neck upward.

A fireman adjusted his helmet. "That's going to be challenging to get down."

They trampled shredded stalks as they entered the demolished cornfield. Brayden walked faster when he found the uprooted maple tree.

"Here," he shouted. "I was right here when I woke up."

The search crew gathered around him. Several people touched the roots of the tree in disbelief. The dogs started to sniff around it.

"Let's fan out in groups of two, making sure at least one person in each group has a cell phone with my number on it, and that I have your number," said the lead police officer. "Search everywhere--even up in trees--until we find her."

Brayden and Dad walked around shrubs stripped of their leaves, and inspected fallen limbs near trees. Brayden even climbed a dense oak tree just beyond the tornado's path, in case Willow was hidden in the branches. They helped another pair of officers flip over splintered boards and warped metal at a demolished gas station, taking over an hour to thoroughly inspect every mound of rubble. Nothing.

"Willow!" they shouted.

Several teams were methodically traipsing through the miles of cornstalks that remained standing. Dad and Brayden were assigned a small area in the northeast corner of the field. They walked up and down each row of corn. Sweat began to pour down their backs, and their arms and legs were scratched from the stalks. Brayden held his head occasionally while they walked. The pain was intensifying in the heat.

"Willow!" they yelled over and over.

"We should rest for a minute," Dad finally said. "Have a drink of water." He handed Brayden a plastic bottle.

Brayden took a deep gulp, handed Dad the bottle and started walking again.

"Hold on, there," Dad said. "You've had a major head injury. You can't keep pushing like this."

"We have to. Do you think I could actually sit down, knowing Willow is still out there?"

"I just don't want you killing yourself in the process. Will you at least stop if you start feeling light-headed or dizzy?"

Brayden nodded, but he was already feeling dizzy. He kept walking.

"Willow!"

Dad stopped suddenly and put his hand on Brayden's shoulder. "Wait! Do you hear something?"

Brayden stopped. A dog was barking in the distance. The bark was deep and persistent. Could it be one of the German Shepherds? Brayden's scalp tingled and the hairs on his arms stood straight up.

Without a word, they began to barrel through the cornfield in the direction of the barking. Cornstalks smacked their faces and they struggled to keep their footing. The barking intensified. A large crowd was gathering on the southern side of the cornfield.

Dad's phone rang.

Brayden's heart began to pound. Had they found her? Was she okay?

"Hello?" Dad said. He stood quietly for a minute that seemed to stretch on for hours. He dropped to his knees. "I see. Thanks, officer."

"Dad?"

"They found her. But she—"

Brayden started running again toward the crowd. He was too excited to process relief.

"Brayden, stop! Let me finish! We need to talk!"

Brayden hurtled forward. His head throbbed and his legs burned but he kept going until he joined the group. His chest heaved up and down as he struggled to catch his breath.

"Where is she?" he yelled.

The lead police officer looked up in surprise. He motioned to a fire fighter, who quickly draped a blanket over a small form.

Brayden pushed through the volunteers. "Is that her? Is that Willow? How badly is she hurt?"

Dad came crashing out of the stalks. "Brayden wait! Don't go over there."

Brayden continued walking.

"Stop!" Dad said. "She didn't make it."

Brayden froze.

"What?!"

Dad's face was pale. "Willow died. I just got the call."

All of the oxygen seemed to drain out of Brayden's body. He looked at the fireman next to the blanket. "You're sure?"

He nodded. "I'm so sorry."

Brayden rubbed the sides of his head, avoiding the bandages. He struggled to remain upright. "Can you tell...When did she die? Did she...suffer all night waiting for us? If I had found her right away, would she have made it?"

"She must have been struck in the head by flying debris while she was in the tornado. She probably died before she even hit the ground."

Brayden nodded. He tried holding back the tears, but gave up. He didn't care who saw him. What did it matter? Nothing mattered anymore.

Dad walked up beside him and wrapped him in his arms. Brayden hugged him back for a moment, and then broke free.

"Can I see her?"

Dad touched his shoulder. "Brayden, are you sure you want—"

"I need to see her."

The fireman and crowd stepped back as Brayden stepped forward and kneeled by his sister. Dad knelt beside him. Brayden stared at the tiny form and froze.

"Dad, can you...I can't seem to..."

Dad leaned forward and pulled back the gray, wool blanket. Willow's crumpled body looked so tiny. So still.

He gasped, grabbing at any air he could suck in. The truth exploded inside him, blowing shrapnel into his heart and soul. His sister was dead. He buried his face in his dad's shoulder. They both sobbed while the crowd dispersed. An ambulance came. Brayden wasn't sure why. They were too late. They were all too late. If only he could have held on. She was like a kite blowing in the wind, only the wind turned angry and brutal...and deadly.

Two men gently lifted her fragile body onto a stretcher and covered her with the wool blanket once more. They carried her into the ambulance and shut the door. Everyone was gone. Still Brayden and his Dad sat. All of the urgency of the last day drained out of them. What was left? They were each absorbed in their own thoughts, too numb to move. What should they do now? Brayden pictured Willow's still form and then imagined her flying out of his hands. Despair and anger swirled around in his brain.

Finally, Dad stood up. He reached his hand down. Brayden looked up and tried to grasp his hand. He missed.

Puzzled, he tried again, but he was too dizzy to focus on his Dad's hand. The pain in his head was intensifying. He clutched the bandages in agony. He felt off-center and lightheaded.

"Brayden?" Dad bent over him. "Oh, no. I was afraid we were pushing too hard. Let's get you back to the hospital."

He nodded, or at least he thought he nodded. He was too woozy to know. Why couldn't he stand up? His head felt like it would explode and his stomach tightened. The cornfield looked like it was spinning. He closed his eyes. So this was what it was like having a concussion. He didn't think it would be this bad. Or powerful. He squinted.

"I'm dizzy, Dad. Everything is spinning."

"You're right. Everything *is* spinning. It's not just in your head. I've got to get you to the car."

"What?"

Brayden tried to focus. A gust of wind whirled in front of them, sending dust into their eyes. Trampled cornstalks began to twirl. A discarded water bottled shook and spun into the rotation.

Dad heaved Brayden over his shoulders, grunting and groaning all of the way to the car. He threw open the passenger door and helped Brayden sit. Then he ran to the other side of the car and started the engine.

Brayden closed his eyes. Another tornado? Unreal. His heart rate was accelerating. He took a deep breath and tried to calm down.

"Huh," Dad said as he drove.

"What?"

"That was it. There's no wind over here. It must have just been a microburst or something."

Brayden sighed. His head still pounded but the dizziness was subsiding. "I'm feeling a little better. Maybe we can just go home."

Dad shook his head. "No way. You almost passed out. I'm not losing both of my kids. One was too much. You're getting that head examined again."

Brayden sank back in the seat. Head injuries were more serious than he thought. The blow to his head made his world spin. The blow to Willow's head ended her world.

CHAPTER 9

DRAFTY GOWN

This time the painting in Brayden's hospital room was an oak tree by a stream. It was peaceful, but he couldn't help but imagine a battered car in its branches. At least it wasn't a willow tree. Trying to focus on anything besides his sister was hard enough without a reminder right in front of him.

He looked down at his hospital gown and longed for his old t-shirt and jeans. How was wearing a drafty gown going to help the doctor monitor his head?

Dad entered the sterile room and sat down on the navy padded chair. His eyes were red and swollen. "Are you all settled in again?"

"I suppose. The nurse has my IV friend hooked up and I'm wearing a baby blue gown, so I guess I'm good."

"The doctor will be here soon to run some tests. Are you still feeling dizzy?"

"Once in a while. I don't notice it as much just sitting in bed. My head still hurts, but I think it's getting better."

Dad tried to smile. "That's good to hear." He looked at the painting for several minutes. The silence became awkward. "I just told your mom about Willow."

Brayden swallowed. "How did she take the news?"

"Hard. Of course. I expected she would."

"Yeah."

Brayden studied his hands. They were still scraped and sore from looking for Willow through the rubble at the gas station. Another reminder of her death. He looked at his white sheet instead. It felt like he should say something, but he didn't know where to start.

"So, last night I let Banjo outside like you suggested," Dad said. "I don't think he's used to being cooped up all day. I had to clean up several accidents."

"He usually goes out quite a few times during the day."

"I guess that's never been my job before. I'm not used to being the only one at home. You and your sister..." Dad winced. "The rest of you have always taken care of the dog."

"Mom and I will be home soon. You won't have to take care of Banjo on your own much longer," said Brayden.

"I don't think taking care of Banjo is what I'm really dreading. I don't want to be in an empty house. I dread walking past Willow's room and knowing..." Dad stopped.

Brayden bit his lip. He didn't want to cry right now.

"At least I know you and your Mom are coming home. I could have lost all three of you. I'm grateful that *all* of the rooms won't stay empty."

They sat in silence for several minutes.

"I should go let Banjo outside so I don't have more surprises. Is there anything you want me to grab from home?"

"How about something to do? I could use a good distraction. I tried flipping on the TV, but talk shows and soap operas aren't very interesting. How about some of my video games?"

"Or a book? Or some homework?" Dad suggested.

"Yeah. I guess you could get those too. If I get *really* bored I might need them."

Dad nodded and left.

Brayden was back to staring at the tree painting. He grabbed the remote and started flipping through channels."Talk show. Talk show. Soap opera. Commercial. News."

Brayden stopped channel surfing when he saw clips of the tornado on the screen. The video was shaky, zoomed in from far away. He squinted, trying to see their car sucked into the whirling mass, but the video was fuzzy. It was probably by a storm chaser or someone brave or foolish enough not to seek cover. He would have sought shelter if they could have found somewhere safe.

A reporter droned on over the noise of the video. "The death toll from this F5 tornado continues to rise as more bodies are discovered. At this time, nine deaths have been reported, but names have not been released."

Brayden jabbed the off button and threw the remote across the room. It smacked against the wall, forcing the back to pop off and the batteries to spill out.

He swung his legs onto the floor and stood up. His head began to pound and a wave of dizziness passed over him. The floor looked like it was slanted. He swayed, trying to regain his balance.

"I've got you," a familiar voice said. Dark hands guided him back to sitting on the bed. "Looks like you need a little more rest before you try to walk."

Brayden tried to focus on the nurse's face, but everything still looked like it was spinning.

"Just close your eyes and lean back," she said. "I heard you were back. I'm not assigned to your new room, but I had to see how you were doing. And I have someone asking to visit you."

"Who?" Brayden asked, keeping his eyes closed.

"Your mom. She's able to walk with crutches now and is worried about you. I can get her when you feel ready. Looks like right now might not be the best time."

"I was doing fine until I stood up," Brayden said. He opened his eyes. The room settled.

Nurse Fonda looked at the busted remote beside the wall. "Looks like it."

"Oh. That. It slipped."

She nodded. "Did it slip while you were watching anything in particular?"

Brayden looked her in the eyes. Her perceptive comments normally would have made him defensive, but she really seemed to care. "Video from the tornado was on the news. They talked about the death toll. It's hard to think of Willow as a statistic."

"I would have a hard time with that too. Your mom told me about your sister. Hang in there. I know you have a hard road ahead of you, but you're going to make it. I've been there and God saw me through it. He'll help you, too."

"What do you mean? You had a sister sucked up into a tornado and killed?" Brayden couldn't keep the sarcasm out of his voice. "I know you mean well, but you don't understand."

"No, I don't fully understand. I didn't have a sister die in a tornado. But I do understand about losing someone you love." She patted his leg and limped to the door.

"Wait. Don't go yet," Brayden said. "Who did you lose?"

Fonda returned to his bed and sat at his feet. "Are you sure you want to hear my story?"

He nodded.

She adjusted the v-neck of her smiley-face covered scrubs and cleared her throat. "My kids and I were in a car accident. I was driving home from my daughter's school musical. Jamal and Neveah sat in the back. It was dark and raining hard. A drunk driver forgot to turn on his headlights and swerved into our lane. He was like our own tornado--he seemed to come from nowhere. It happened so fast...I couldn't get out of his way in time. Both of my children died. I was stuck in the hospital for a while, but here I am. A car wreck couldn't get rid of me. Even a *tornado* couldn't stop you. You're going to get through this tough time. It will get better."

"I hope so," Brayden said.

"Hope is a good thing." Fonda smiled. "Are you ready for a visit from your mom? She really wants to see you."

Brayden nodded.

"I'll be right back." She shuffled to the door. Brayden noticed her limp again and wondered if that was from her accident. She seemed so happy. He never would have guessed she had gone through so much pain.

A few minutes later, Fonda's cheerful face peeked back in the door. "Look who's here."

Mom hopped into the room on her crutches. She was still clumsy with them, but was able to get to his bed by herself. She gave him a hug and kissed the top of his head.

"Hey, Mom."

"Dad told me you pushed too hard yesterday and had a set-back. Are you okay now? Are you still dizzy? How is your head?" she asked. Worry cast shadows on her face.

"I'm fine."

Fonda paused as she headed to the door.

Brayden clarified. "I mean, I still get dizzy if I get out of bed, but while I'm sitting I'm fine."

Fonda smiled at him as she closed the door behind her.

Mom crossed her arms. "We should never have allowed you to go looking for your sister. Not with a head injury."

"I had to, Mom. I couldn't just sit here, not knowing if she needed us, not knowing whether...she was alive or...not."

Mom's eyes watered. "Not knowing was hard." She sat silently for a few moments. "I suppose if you hadn't helped the teams, they might still be searching for Willow. *I* didn't even know you landed so far from me."

"The wind tossed us around like...like we were trash." He didn't even try to disguise the bitter edge to his voice.

Mom hugged him again. "I'm so glad I didn't lose you, too. This is all just...too much. I still feel like it's my fault the tornado caught us."

Brayden felt pressure building in his head again. He needed to talk about something else. Anything else. "So how's your leg?"

"Better. I've been practicing with my crutches."

"I saw that. Not bad. How long will you have to stay in here?"

"A few more days. I hope you will be able to leave about the same time."

"I wish I could leave now. I don't know how much longer I can stare at the same painting. My buddies are probably wondering where I am."

Mom's jaw dropped. "I completely forgot to call the school to let them know why you've been gone and when you'll be back. I need to call Willow's school too, and tell them..." Her voice cracked. "Tell them she won't ever be back."

"I don't want to go back either," Brayden said. "There are only a few weeks left. I don't want to have to explain what happened. I'm not ready to deal with everyone." The pain in his head intensified. He closed his eyes and rubbed his bandages.

Mom leaned forward. "Is the dizziness back? Do I need to call the doctor? Can I do something to help?"

"I just don't want to talk about this anymore." He opened his eyes. The room started to spin. He groaned.

"I'm getting the doctor. He was supposed to run more tests on you this afternoon anyhow."

She pressed a red button on the side of the bed. Several minutes later, a nurse appeared. Mom explained her concerns and the nurse left again. Ten minutes later, she returned with the doctor.

"It looks like it's time to run a few more tests," the doctor said, flipping through pages in Brayden's chart. "I know we already did some testing, but it wouldn't hurt to do them again since you are still having so much pain and dizziness."

The nurse helped Brayden sit in a wheelchair and pushed him into a different room. She tested his vision, hearing, balance, coordination, reflexes, memory, and concentration. Brayden studied her face after each test to see how he had done, but she maintained a bland expression that gave him no clues. He missed Fonda's smile and honesty. She would tell it to him straight.

After the last test, he waited for reassurance. Nothing. Finally, he asked, "So, how did I do?"

The nurse looked over her papers. "Decent. I'll have the doctor see what he thinks. You can hop back into the wheelchair."

He hopped twice in response, but it aggravated his headache. The nurse remained stoic and wheeled him back to his room. Mom was still sitting by the bed, flipping through TV channels. She hobbled out of her chair and helped him back into his bed.

"How did it go?"

"Decent," Brayden said, trying to imitate the robotic nurse.

The nurse did not seem to notice and did not elaborate. "I'll have the doctor talk to you soon." She clipped the test results to his chart and bustled out the door.

"I wish Fonda was still assigned to you," Mom said.

The doctor returned and stood at the foot of the bed, reviewing the results. "Well, Mrs. Kesler, Brayden is evidently improving, except when it comes to his balance, coordination and vision. I think we'll have him go ahead and do a CT scan just to be safe."

Brayden sat up straighter. "I've heard of a CT scan, but I'm not really sure what it is. Does it hurt?"

"No." The doctor smiled. "You'll lie still on a table that will slide through a doughnut-shaped X-ray machine. It will take multiple cross-sectional pictures that will give us two-dimensional images of your skull and brain. It should only take about ten minutes. After facing a tornado and getting stitches in your head, this will seem easy."

Brayden nodded. "I didn't catch that middle part of what you said, but a donut X-ray machine sounds like something I can handle. Can we do it now so I can go home?"

"I'm guessing it's too late for tonight. We'll try to get you in early tomorrow."

Mom patted Brayden's arm. "I'll call your school once we get the CT results, so I can let them know if you will be returning soon."

Brayden scowled. "Now I don't know what test results to hope for."

CHAPTER 10

SUN AND RAINBOWS

The next morning, Brayden was grateful when a bell chimed and he was pulled out of the CT scan. It was harder holding still in an enclosed place than he thought. He had to fight the urge to thrash out with his arms and legs. The stoic nurse wheeled him back to his room and stopped suddenly.

Dad was sprawled out on the hospital bed, snoring at full volume. He had kicked one of his brown loafers off and his arm flopped over the side.

"I've got this," Brayden told the nurse. "You can go."

She shrugged and left. Brayden wheeled his chair up to the side of the bed and grabbed his glass of water off the side table. He stuck his hand in the water and let water drip off his fingers onto his dad's face.

Dad twitched and snorted.

"Oh, Dad. Wake up." Brayden let a few more drops fall.

Dad rubbed them off with his sleeve but kept snoring.

Brayden poured the remaining water onto his dad's face. "Wake up."

Dad sputtered and snapped upright. "What's going on?"

"You're in the hospital. Sleeping. On my bed."

Dad blinked in confusion for a moment and dried his face with the white sheet. "I was going to sit in the chair to wait for you, but I guess I was just too tired." He yawned. "Was the water really necessary?"

"No." Brayden grinned. "But it was fun."

"Fun for you." Dad swung his legs off the bed and helped Brayden climb under the covers. "So? Any results?"

Brayden shook his head. "Not yet. In the meantime, I get to hang out here, enjoying the great food and entertainment."

"Sounds like you don't need anything I brought from home then. No big deal. I can just take it with me when I leave." He stretched and crammed his foot back into his shoe.

"Hold on, there, Dad. Let's not be hasty. I might be able to handle a few more things to do. What do you have?"

Dad walked over to the chair and grabbed a bright blue duffel bag. "I have some of your homework."

"Ugh."

"And some books."

"Sort of ugh."

"A couple games we could play."

"Better."

"And your video games."

Brayden sat up. "Now we're talking. Bring them on over."

Dad leaned back in the navy chair and crossed his arms. "I'd be glad to--once you've done some homework."

"I actually have to do homework at a time like this? Doesn't being in the hospital earn me some time off?"

"Yes. Several days of it. But now you're bored and odds are you'll be back in school soon—"

"That is yet to be determined. Mom said we wouldn't make any decisions until I got my test results back."

"Well, in the meantime, you can start some homework. I couldn't find your backpa—"

"It was in the car, so you probably never will."

"Good point. But I did find your math and history books that were tossed on your bedroom floor. Your video games can wait until you're alone."

"So do you need to go check on Mom?"

"Yes. But I'll read in here first to make sure you get your homework done." Dad picked up the bag and dropped it on the bed. He returned to the chair, settling in with his reading glasses on and a book open.

"I seem to have misplaced my pencil."

"Nice try. I stuck three pencils and some paper in the bag."

Sensing this was an argument he would not win, Brayden dug out his Algebra II book and began working problems. His brain was sluggish and couldn't focus for very long, but the homework was a good distraction. Not that he would ever admit that to his dad. He zoned out repeatedly, fell asleep at least once, and had to ask for help from his dad a few times, but he finally managed to complete an assignment.

"How about a game break?" he asked, stuffing the math book into the duffel bag.

"Sure. I brought a deck of cards and some checkers."

"I meant a video game."

"I'm guessing you have homework in more than one subject. No video games until it's all done."

"That will take too long. In case you didn't notice, my brain isn't quite up to speed. How about showing some compassion?" Brayden exhibited his best pathetic expression.

"I'd be glad to—but not by giving you video games. They won't help your brain heal."

"Okay. Then a checker break. Beating you might cheer me up."

"Hope you don't mind staying sad, then."

They played three games. Brayden only managed to win one time, and even then he suspected that Dad made a few mistakes on purpose. After the games, he pulled out his World History book. He had barely begun the assignment when his eyes started to get heavy. Hours later, he woke up and found a drool puddle on his notebook. The chair was empty, but a note was on his game system on the pillow. It said, "You earned this."

Brayden shuffled over to the chair and jammed his History book into his bag. He clutched the electronic device to his chest and sighed. After making himself as comfortable as possible in bed, he escaped into his game until noon.

The nurse carried in a tan plastic tray that emitted a foul smell, arranged it on his sliding table, checked his stats and left.

"I'm having a good day. Thanks!" Brayden called after her.

He removed the tray lid. A small bowl was filled with brown, lumpy stew. Canned peaches were in another compartment on the tray, but had spilled into some faded peas. Two plastic wrapped crackers had fallen into a bright pink substance that he suspected was pudding. He unwrapped a spoon and scooped up some stew. He managed to get a chunk of potato and mystery meat and took a bite. It was luke-warm, but he was so hungry he still ate it. At this point, even bad food was better than nothing.

Mom and Dad entered the room just as he was finishing the pink pudding.

"I hope your food was better than mine," Mom commented.

"Probably not, but I was hungry."

"That's a good sign," she said. She scooted his video games to the foot of the bed so she could sit beside him instead of in her wheelchair. "Did you finish your homework?"

"No. But I started it. I'm not exactly thinking at turbo speed. Is it possible my brain got sucked into the tornado?" Brayden asked.

"Not funny. Are you feeling any better?" Mom asked. She stroked back his hair, avoiding his bandages. A frown deepened the lines in her forehead.

"Maybe a little. Okay, Mom. You look rattled. What's up?"

She sighed. "You know me too well. The doctor got the test results back while you were sleeping. He seemed rather...well, unsure of the findings."

"What's that supposed to mean?"

"He said it was like you were moving around during the scan," Dad answered. "The pictures aren't clear."

"I held perfectly still," Brayden protested.

"That's what the technician said. He didn't notice you moving around." Mom put her hand on Brayden's arm reassuringly. "I'm sure you did your best. The doctor just thinks we need to try again. He can't make a diagnosis with blurry images. This time they may add some contrast dye to make it easier to read."

Brayden rolled his eyes. "So when do I have to test again?"

"Actually, now would be good," Mom said. "We'll go with you. I wish we could go into the room with you, but we'll be just outside the door."

Fonda appeared at the door a few minutes later. Today she was wearing scrubs depicting sunbursts and rainbows. "I guess I've been checking on you and your family too much. They finally just assigned me to your room again."

"I'm glad," Brayden said.

"That makes two of us." She helped him into the wheelchair and turned to face his parents. "Do you want to follow us?"

They nodded.

"Well, let's get this show on the road. You need to find out what's percolating in that head of yours."

She wheeled him back to the CT scanner. He waved good-bye to his parents as a technician with an identification tag labeled "Larry" led him into a bare room and helped him back onto the table. This time the straps holding his head seemed tighter. The room was cool and the table was hard, but Brayden was determined not to move.

Larry inserted an IV into the top of Brayden's hand. A dye started pumping through the line, making him feel warm and flushed. He noticed a metallic taste in his mouth and longed for a drink of water. Larry carefully removed the bandages from Brayden's head and tossed them into the trash can. The table slid into the round opening of the scanner. Brayden closed his eyes and held still, not even risking taking a breath. The scanner clicked and buzzed as it took pictures. The table slid back out.

"Good job," Larry said. "I'm *sure* you didn't move that time."

"I hope the doctor agrees with you," said Brayden.

Fonda returned and wrapped his head with fresh bandages. "We don't want to scare people by exposing your Frankenstein stitches just yet." She wheeled him back down the hall.

"How did you do, honey?" asked Mom.

"Still as a statue," Brayden answered.

"Good. I called the school and told them..." she swallowed painfully, "...told them everything. Dad is going to pick up the work you've missed. I told them you would be back as soon as the doctor gave his approval."

"Maybe I should have moved during the CT scan after all."

"You are hilarious. You've got to go back sooner or later."

"Later would be good."

Dad pushed Mom in her wheelchair to her room so she could take a nap, and he drove to the high school for homework. Brayden didn't mind being left alone. It meant more time vegetating with a zombie game.

The new CT results finally came in the next afternoon. The doctor gathered the family together in Brayden's hospital room.

"I studied the second set of CT scans. The dye was a good idea, but the scans are still very...unclear."

"I'm sure I held still," Brayden protested. "I don't have to do the scan again, do I?"

"The technician confirmed that you were motionless, so no, I don't think another scan will be helpful. Both scans show a foggy area around your brain. Your brain is also swollen, but that can be expected with a severe blow to the head. I didn't find any foreign objects or noticeable bleeding, so I don't think surgery would be helpful."

"No surgery. I'm all for that," Brayden said.

The doctor turned to Mr. and Mrs. Kesler. "But I do think that we need to keep him here a few more days for observation. The hazy area around his brain is concerning me. It's just not normal, even after a major head blow."

"Maybe it *is* normal after being sucked into a tornado," Brayden suggested. "I mean, how many cases have they really studied about brain injuries from whirling around in an F5 tornado?"

"True," the doctor agreed. "Let's just give you a few more days of observation to be safe."

So Brayden stayed. Mom was released with strict instruction to use crutches and elevate her leg as much as possible. She and Dad still spent most of the weekend at the hospital to be with Brayden. They supervised him attempting homework. They also played games, and watched TV with him. Any time they tried to talk about Willow or the tornado, Brayden changed the subject. Not only did the discussions make his heart ache, they made his head pound.

Early Monday morning, Fonda peeked into Brayden's room. "Oh, good. You're awake. No Mom or Dad yet?"

"Dad is trying to return to work today. Mom should be up in an hour or so."

"Do you have socks?" she asked.

"Socks?" Brayden gave her a strange look. "I guess so. Why?"

"Because I want you to put them on. We're going for a walk down the halls."

"For more tests?"

"No." Fonda put her hands on her wide hips. "We need to get you moving. You've been in this hospital bed too long."

"I get up by myself to go to the bathroom."

"Do you still get woozy?"

"No."

"Good. Then it's time to walk a little further. We need to make sure you'll be okay if you go home soon. So, let's see you get up and find those socks."

Brayden stood up slowly, leery of a head rush. He dug through a bag of clothes on the chair until he found some old white tube socks and pulled them on.

"Any dizziness?" Fonda asked.

"Not yet."

"Then grab my arm and let's go for a stroll. If your head starts pounding or you get dizzy, let me know."

"Got it."

Oddly enough, he did not feel awkward holding her arm. She smiled reassuringly as they walked down the hall. Her head only reached his shoulder and he noticed her slight limp, but she managed to keep him steady and propel him forward. She gave him a tour of the hospital, telling stories about some of her favorite patients. Whenever his head started to hurt, they would find a chair and relax for a moment. They talked about his high school football team, the Kansas City Chiefs, the hospital food, food they actually liked at favorite restaurants, and his dog, Banjo. Brayden was actually disappointed when they returned to his hospital room.

Fonda filled up his water glass while he climbed back into bed. Mom hobbled in the door on her crutches.

"Good timing. We just got back from a walk," Brayden said.

"Really? How did it go?"

"He did great," Fonda said. "We walked for nearly an hour, with just short stops along the way. If he can do that well for a few more walks, I think the doctor will let him go home. Maybe the two of you can take an afternoon stroll."

"Sounds good," Mom said.

"Back to my rounds. Thanks for the walk, Brayden. If I spent all of my breaks that way, I'd be so skinny you'd have trouble finding me."

"Some people are worth looking for," he said.

Fonda smiled wider than the smiley faces decorating her scrubs. "You'd better watch out, Mrs. Kesler. He knows how to sweet talk. He'll be sweeping some girl off her feet any day now."

Brayden pictured Kenzie's scowling face. "I don't know about that. I seem to get it all wrong with most girls. You just bring out the best in me."

CHAPTER 11

WIND THRASHING

By Tuesday afternoon, Brayden completed three more walks. The doctor signed Brayden's release papers, but reminded him to return in two weeks to have stitches removed, or earlier if he noticed prolonged dizziness or head pain.

Brayden climbed into their car, eager to get home. Several miles down the road, his excitement waned. Scars from the tornado made his stomach churn. Power lines were back up, but the trees were bare and disfigured. A strip of houses had been transformed into piles of drywall and concrete, and several stores were still missing shingles or an entire roof. Brayden's insulated bubble from the hospital popped and pain washed over him. It spread to his head, and he rubbed his temples.

"Are you okay back there?" asked Mom.

"Yeah." He knew his voice was not very convincing.

He envisioned the wind thrashing trees and plucking cars off the road and...

"Brayden? Do we need to go back?" Dad asked.

"No. Keep going. I'll be fine."

He closed his eyes until the pain subsided. By the time he looked out the window again, there were only a few broken branches and cracked windows.

Dad pressed a button and the garage door closed behind them. Brayden didn't move.

"Did I ever ask whether our house was hit by the tornado?" he asked.

"Maybe not directly, but I told you our neighborhood was barely touched," Dad said.

Brayden gritted his teeth and got out of the car. He could already hear Banjo howling inside. As soon as he stepped through the door, his dog started jumping up and down on him, howling and wagging his tail.

"I missed you, too," Brayden said. He bent down to pat the dog's brown and white back and scratch behind his ears. Banjo licked his face and hands.

"Can I help you up the stairs?" asked Mom.

Brayden eyed her crutches. "I think Dad's the safer choice for now."

She tapped her forehead. "Of course."

He held onto the railing with one hand and Dad's shoulder with the other. Banjo wove between them as they climbed each stair, nearly tripping both of them. Brayden paused to catch his breath at the top before they shuffled down the hall.

He hesitated when they approached Willow's room. Her door was open and everything was exactly how she left it Wednesday morning. His head began to pound and he squeezed Dad's arm as a wave of dizziness washed over him. Dad guided him past her room and into his own.

"I'm going to crash for a while," Brayden said, flopping onto his bed.

Mom hobbled in. "If you need anything, let me know." She filled his glass with water and adjusted his blinds while Dad propped the backpack up against the wall. They slipped quietly out of the room.

Brayden stared at the wall for several minutes until his head stopped throbbing. He rolled over and grabbed a video game, needing a distraction to block thoughts about Willow's empty room.

"Time to eat!" Mom called

Brayden jolted awake and rubbed his eyes. Banjo was curled up beside him on the blanket. The smell of garlic, tomato sauce and fresh bread filled the house. His stomach rumbled. Real food. It was enough to get out of bed. He carefully drifted downstairs.

Mom was cutting homemade lasagna into squares with a long knife. She scooped each serving onto white dinner plates with cheese stretching and sauce dripping. Brayden's mouth watered. He grabbed a fat slice of garlic bread and took a crunchy bite.

"Wait until we pray," Mom said, but she smiled.

Dad poured ice and water into four glasses and started to place one by each plate. He paused a moment and carried one glass back to the sink and dumped it. Brayden gripped the table but pretended not to notice.

Mom prayed and then watched Brayden take a huge bite of lasagna. "I'm glad to see you enjoying your food again."

"Thanks for making my favorite meal," he said with his mouth full. "It tastes even better after a week of hospital food."

"Really? I kind of miss the mushy peas and instant mashed potatoes," Mom said.

Dad closed his eyes and grinned as he chewed. "I may have a hard time going without peanut butter and jelly sandwiches for every meal."

"That's really what you ate all the time we were gone?" asked Mom.

"Well, not for every meal. I had cold cereal for breakfast."

"That's pathetic." Mom shook her head.

"Yeah, Dad," Brayden agreed.

"Oh. And I suppose you could do better?"

"Yes. When you and Mom have a date night, I cook great macaroni and cheese. Just ask Willow." Brayden swallowed hard, catching what he said.

The joking around ended abruptly. It was nice while it lasted. Each family member avoided eye contact and ate in silence for several minutes.

Finally, Mom spoke up. "While we are all thinking about Willow, there is something we've been needing to talk to you about."

"What?"

"When we found out you could be released from the hospital today, we made some calls to family and friends. We scheduled Willow's funeral for tomorrow at 2:00."

Brayden dropped his fork. "Tomorrow? So soon? I just got home today. I'm not ready for her funeral."

"I know it seems sudden," said Dad. "But she died almost a week ago and we had to set something up with the funeral home. We put it off because we wanted you to be able to go, but now you can."

"Your grandparents and most of our other family said they could come tomorrow. We need to say our good-byes. We need some closure." Mom squeezed Brayden's arm.

He jerked his arm away. "I'm not ready for closure. I can't just say good-bye and forget she ever existed."

"Oh, honey. We know that. We don't want you to ever forget her." Tears rolled down Mom's cheeks. "We just want to honor her and start the grieving process."

"Do I have to say anything at the funeral?"

"Only if you want to," Mom said.

"Though you might regret it later if you don't," Dad added.

"I don't know if I can do it."

"You can write it down," Mom suggested. "That might make it easier."

"Are both of you going to say something at the funeral?"

Mom and Dad nodded.

Brayden stared at his fork. "I don't know what to say. I've only been to one funeral before--you know, for Uncle Jack--and that was a long time ago. I don't remember what anyone said."

"I can help you if you want," Mom volunteered. "I wrote down what I'm going to say in case I get too choked up and my mind goes blank."

"I'll think about it." Brayden tried to take another bite of lasagna, but it no longer tasted good. He swirled the fork in the cheese. "Can we change subjects?"

"Sure," Dad said.

They all sat quietly, picking at their food.

"So...work was good today," Dad finally said.

"That's nice," Mom replied without looking up.

"I saw Trey and Max when I was taking Banjo for a walk last night. They were asking about you and wanted to know when you were going back to school. What do you think?" asked Dad.

"About what?"

"About when you will go back to school," Dad clarified.

"Next year," Brayden said. "Can't I just keep doing the work from home?"

Mom shook her head. "We've already discussed this. I don't think it will be good for you to avoid school. You need to be with your friends and have something else to think about. Besides, we already told your teachers that you would be back later this week."

"I don't want to be around anyone yet. They won't understand."

"Then help them understand. Tell them what happened," Mom said.

"But I don't want to talk about it anymore. It just makes it worse."

"How about taking one more day off," Dad said.

"One more day? Seriously? That's it? We're going to be at the funeral tomorrow. That's not a day off. I get home from the hospital today, I have to speak in my dead sister's funeral tomorrow and I have to go back to school the next day?" Brayden shouted. "No problem. That sounds like an easy week to me. Can I have a week like this again some time?"

"I went back to work this week," said Dad. "Do you think that was easy for me? Willow's death is hard on all of us."

"Can I at least take the rest of the week off?"

"Don't you think you could at least go to school this Friday?" Mom asked. "That way you could ease into the routine."

Brayden started to rub his temples. "I'm not ready. It's all just too much."

Mom and Dad exchanged looks. Mom sighed. "Okay. You can wait until Monday. But then no more arguments. I'm not having you miss the last two weeks of school."

"Got it." Brayden started breathing easier. "Can I bike to and from school by myself so I can get there at the last minute and leave right when school is over?"

"If you think that will help," said Mom. She looked down at the cast on her leg. "I guess it's not like *I* can bike with you."

"Yeah. May I be excused?"

"But you didn't finish your lasagna. And I have brownies for dessert," Mom protested.

"Maybe I'll eat a brownie tomorrow. I need time to think about the funeral."

"But you..." Dad put his hand on Mom's arm and she stopped.

Brayden pushed in his chair and climbed the stairs. When he reached Willow's room he paused and looked inside again. It would be easier to pretend she was away at camp. The funeral was too soon. He wasn't ready to talk about her death. He wasn't ready for her to be dead.

He turned and trudged to his room. A stack of lined paper sat on his desk next to a sharpened pencil. He sat in the chair and stared at the blank sheets. Willow was the writer in the family, not him. He pictured her with her purple notebook, writing stories and drawing pictures. The pencil taunted him, rolling across the paper. He snatched it and snapped it in two. He was going to bed.

CHAPTER 12

FLOOD OF TEARS

The next morning, Mom knocked timidly on the door. "Brayden? Are you awake?"

Brayden rolled over.

"Would you like some breakfast? I made you french toast."

He loved french toast. "I'll be down in a minute." He saw the paper and broken pencil on his desk and remembered what the day held. "Actually, I'm not hungry."

"You need to eat."

"No, thanks."

"Can I come in for a minute?" she asked.

"I guess."

Mom opened the door and maneuvered her crutches so she could sit on the edge of his bed. "I know today will be hard, but we can get through it together."

Brayden stared up at the ceiling. His throat tightened. "I can't handle it. And I don't just mean the funeral. I can't handle us being caught in the tornado. Or Willow slipping through my fingers. I can't handle finding out she's dead.

None of it seems real. None of it *should be* real. I want to undo it. I need to make it right."

Mom wrapped her arms around him. "I wish we *could* undo it. I'd do anything to decide to get Willow's reed another day. Or to stay in the music store until the tornado passed. I mentally beat myself up about that all the time. I wish I could have seen into the future and known that tornado was coming. But I didn't. And now Willow's gone and it seems wrong." She paused, struggling to contain her tears. "But we can't give up. We have to take one day at a time, and today we need to have the funeral. And this morning you need to decide what to say for her. And right now, you need to eat."

"What's the point?"

"The point is, your bottomless pit of a stomach is empty and my job is to fill it--or at least try to fill it. So let's start with that, and then we'll tackle the rest. I'll meet you downstairs."

Brayden soaked in her words. He reluctantly left his room and sat at the kitchen table. Mom passed him the butter and syrup. He cut off a wedge of butter and smeared it on the french toast, and then he drowned it with a double serving of syrup.

"That's what I like to see," Mom said, smiling.

"You usually complain about how much butter and syrup I use."

"Not today. Dig in."

Brayden managed to eat three slices of french toast and licked his plate clean. Mom washed the dishes before they returned upstairs. She handed him two sheets of paper filled with writing.

"These are my notes for what I want to say at the funeral," she said. "Feel free to read them. Maybe it will help you come up with ideas for what you want to say. You can make yours any length you want."

Brayden nodded and started reading. Mom wrote about holding Willow for the first time in the hospital and marveling that someone so tiny and fragile could bring so much joy. She mentioned Willow's sweet personality, her hugs and kisses, and frequent homemade gifts. He saw tear drops on the paper around the words sharing her writing and artistic potential. The eulogy ended telling about how she had improved all of their lives and how they would be together again someday in heaven.

His heart felt like it was being twisted. How could he write about his sister, when he just wanted to run away and escape it all? His eyes drifted to his digital alarm clock and panic washed over him. There wasn't time to succumb to his selfish needs. He had to start writing. Shockingly, he realized that his dad could be right. He might regret it if he didn't speak at the funeral. He had enough regrets as it was. The blank paper on his desk taunted him. He dug around for a pencil and scribbled down a few sentences. He read them aloud. The words sounded hollow and cheesy, so he wadded up the paper and hurled it into the trash can. After three more attempts, he finally felt like he had written something he could read. Emotionally exhausted, he crawled onto his bed for that long-awaited escape through sleep.

Later that afternoon, Mom woke him for lunch. The idea of eating made his stomach hurt even more.

"I can't eat, Mom. I don't think I can keep anything down."

She stroked his hair. "Actually, I can't eat either. You should probably start getting dressed for the funeral. Dad's home. We're going early, so we'll need to leave in half an hour."

Brayden closed his eyes and inhaled slowly. He pulled on his one pair of black dress pants and a gray button-down shirt. His hair refused to flatten, even after he dunked his head under the faucet, so he spiked it up with gel like usual. He stood in front of the mirror and carefully peeled off his old bandage. The scar was pink and puckered, but no longer oozed. Soon the doctor would remove the blue stitches. He grabbed his fuzzy green washcloth and soaked it with water and soap. After a gentle wash and rinse, he held a skinny strip of gauze on his wound and surrounded it with medical tape.

A heavy cloud hung over the family as they drove to the church. Dad grasped Mom's hand on her left crutch as she managed her way on the sidewalk to the front glass doors. A gentle breeze sent ripples through the red and white flowers clustered by the grass. Brayden pictured his sister skipping along beside him, chattering and eager to see her friends. He kicked a pebble off the sidewalk.

They shuffled through the reception hall into the large colonial-style sanctuary. Willow's 16 X 20 framed portrait was perched on an easel draped in vines and white daisies. She was wearing a purple dress and had her wispy hair pinned to the side. Brayden swallowed hard. Her light blue eyes seemed to be looking right at him.

More daisies filled large glass vases placed strategically around the stage. A little white casket lay to the right. Brayden's heart started beating faster. He was grateful the casket was closed for now.

"Do you want to sit down?" Mom asked. "You look pale."

Brayden nodded and dropped into the front pew. Fog engulfed him, making the entire sanctuary feel unreal. Gentle music began as friends and relatives filed into the pews behind them. Some people talked to him and patted him on the back, but Brayden felt distant and barely noticed their efforts. Mom and Dad eventually sat beside him.

Their pastor welcomed everyone, but his words did not register. Brayden was miles away in his mind. Family and friends sang some of Willow's favorite hymns and choruses. Brayden tried to join in, but his throat was tight and not much sound came out. He glanced at his mom. She kept dabbing the corners of her eyes, but her make-up had already washed away. Dad blew his nose repeatedly.

Three of Willow's band friends played a trio on their clarinets. Pastor read 2 Corinthians 1:3-5 from the Bible and gave a short message. Brayden choked back sobs as Mom and Dad took turns sharing their thoughts about Willow. It took all of his concentration just to keep repairing the chinks in the levee before a floodgate of tears burst through. The room grew quiet. Was someone calling his name? Finally Dad helped him to his feet and walked him up to the small podium.

Brayden contemplated returning to his seat. How could he possibly manage a single sentence right now? He forced his eyes up beyond the podium to the audience. When had so many people arrived? Crowds did not bother him. He usually liked being the center of attention. But today he was at risk of blubbering like a baby. He took a deep breath and pulled out his notes. His head began to pound and his fingers shook, but he managed to start reading.

"Willow was my little sister. I'm sure I wasn't always the best brother. I teased her and fought with her, but it kind of seemed like my job. The thing was..." He wiped his eyes with his shirt sleeve. "The thing was, I liked when she followed me around, or tried to do what I did. She was good at making me do things I was too old to do. She would somehow talk me into digging in the mud, playing with her stuffed animals, running in the rain, flying kites..." Brayden felt his throat constricting, but stubbornly continued. "I love her and wish I could have held onto her longer in the tornado..." His eyes blurred and he couldn't read his notes. He held his head, trying to ease the pain so he could finish. Finally, he felt Dad's hand on his shoulder and he was guided back to the front pew.

The fog returned as they sang another song and the Pastor led them in a final prayer. Somehow, he walked with his family past Willow's casket. It was open now. They paused for a moment, each placing a daisy on her folded hands. Huge sobs racked his body. He tried to contain them, certain that he was being watched, but he failed. Mom wrapped her arm around his shoulders and handed him a Kleenex. She and Dad had tears pouring down their cheeks.

Brayden looked away from the casket. This wasn't how he wanted to remember her. She didn't wear makeup yet. Curls never lasted in her hair. She only held still when she was sleeping. His eyes sought the photograph of her and he focused on that instead.

He vaguely remembered leaving the church, following the black hearse that led the funeral procession to the cemetery. His personal haze blended with the storm clouds. A muted rumble of thunder greeted them, but the wind was uncharacteristically still. Did it regret the part it played in Willow's death?

They gathered around a gravesite with family while rain dripped onto hats and combed hair. Dad removed his reading glasses once he realized they were too wet for him to see through. Mom's purple scarf was getting wet. Did she wear it because it was Willow's favorite color? He should have worn a purple tie.

The pastor's mouth was moving. What was he saying? Brayden strained to listen but he could not focus. The white casket was gently placed into the ground. Rain rolled off the smooth surface. How did the casket get here? Who carried it? Someone was scooping dirt onto the casket. The soil mixed with the rain, clumping into mud. Willow would like to play in the mud, but she wouldn't want to be buried in it. Why hadn't they cremated her instead? She shouldn't be trapped in the earth. His sister was light and laughter. She should be floating on the breeze, flitting through trees and dancing over flowers. Why hadn't he asked what was going to happen to her? Why hadn't he treated her better? Why hadn't he held on?

Windshield wipers methodically vacillated on low settings. Headlights gleamed. The next thing he knew, they were back in their house, but it was full of people. Too many people. Tissues were in so many hands, wiping eyes, blowing noses. Endless chatter flowed from room to room. Crockpots and casseroles and plastic containers of random entrees covered the counter. The smell of fried chicken collided with the aroma of chili, topped with the scent of roast beef. Rolls and cookies and pies were stacked on the kitchen table. The walls seemed to close in. There wasn't enough room to breathe. Brayden's stomach churned.

Mom and Dad had fake smiles accompanying their red eyes and tear-streaked faces. They were talking and hugging family and friends, and being sucked further and further away from him. Brayden eyed the stairs. Maybe no one would notice if he slipped away. His whole body felt like a washcloth that was wrung out too tight. He craved the solitude of his room, and inched closer to the stair case. Grandma Kesler intercepted him and gave him a hug. She smelled like gardenias and menthol. Her perfume stung his nose, forcing him to sneeze. What was she saying to him? Words of wisdom? Words of comfort? He tried to smile and nod, but had a feeling he failed.

Uncle Mark gave him a side hug. Aunt Carrie smothered him in a full embrace. He tried to hug her in return, but his arms weren't long enough. When had she become so...wide? Her padded arms reminded him of pale pink pillows. He longed to disappear to his room and go to bed.

Cousins of all ages threaded their way through the adults. Sarah and James found the cookies on the table and started to help themselves. Their mom spotted them and chased them away. Nick sneaked upstairs and released Banjo from his crate. The beagle bayed and barked at everyone in the house, smacking them with his wagging tail.

"Can you put him back in his crate?" Dad asked.

Brayden nodded. Here was his chance. He chased Banjo around the room, accidentally running into Grandpa Kesler, who tried to start a conversation. He nodded politely for a few minutes before grabbing his dog by the collar. Banjo licked his hand and then whined to be released. Brayden drug the wriggling, barking beast to the stairs but finally decided it would be easier just to carry him. He heaved the overweight beagle into his arms and hauled him to the crate. Banjo whined as Brayden shoved him behind the wire door and latched it.

"Sorry, boy."

He crept to his room, anticipating time alone, but made a detour when he heard laughter. Three more cousins were playing in Willow's room. Brayden's face flushed and his head pounded.

"You don't belong in here," he said.

"But we want to play," Maxeen said. She finished placing tea cups in a circle on the floor.

"Play downstairs."

"There's nothing to do downstairs," Avery said. She squeezed Willow's sock monkey, and gave him a cup of tea.

"Put that down," Brayden commanded.

"What? The monkey or the cup?"

"Both."

"Why? I won't break them."

"Because they are Willow's."

"She wouldn't mind if we played with her stuff," said Josh.

"Well, I do, so leave before I get your mom."

"Go ahead," said Josh crossing his arms.

Brayden clenched his fists, fighting the urge to grab them and toss them out the door. "Okay. But be careful while I'm gone."

"Why?" asked Maxeen. She adjusted the straw hat on Willow's bear.

"Because I just saw Willow's ghost peek out of her closet."

They screamed and shoved each other, racing downstairs. He watched them return to the chaos on the main floor before he returned to Willow's room to restore her tea set and stuffed animals to their rightful places. Satisfied with his work, he slipped inside his bedroom and locked the door. He grabbed a pill from his medicine bottle, and washed it down with dusty water from the glass on his side table. The talking downstairs was loud, even with his door closed, so he grabbed his ear buds, stuck them in and turned on some music. The pounding in his head finally started to subside. He closed his eyes and curled onto his bed, letting the fog finally envelope him.

CHAPTER 13

ICE QUEEN

The next few days dragged by. Brayden rarely left his room. Mom and Dad took turns checking on him, trying to get him to talk. They invited him on walks and bike rides, but he refused.

"Talking makes my head hurt," he said. "Sleeping makes it feel better."

Piles of dirty clothes littered his room. His mom finally forced him to throw them in the laundry basket. He stuffed smelly t-shirts and socks into the hamper. Hidden under a pair of denim shorts was a crumpled triangle, painted with footballs and a gecko.

"The kite Willow made," he whispered.

He untangled the long tail and rerolled the string. Maybe it *was* time to get out of his room. He dug through his drawer until he found a pair of socks that were actually clean. He jammed them on his feet, along with a pair of old sneakers. He trotted down the stairs.

"I'll be in the front," he called over his shoulder.

His mom followed him to the door. "I'm glad," she said.

He looked up and down the street. A young mother with a haggard expression ambled by, pushing a fussy baby in a black stroller. Two neighbor kids wrestled in the grass. Brayden hid the kite behind his back until they ran to their backyards.

Convinced no one was watching, he held the kite up as far as he could stretch and then let go, pulling on the string. It plummeted to the sidewalk. Brayden repeated the process two more times. The wind refused to keep the kite in the air.

"Oh, so *now* you won't blow?" Brayden yelled. He shook the kite in the air. "You can't get a tiny kite in the air, but you can rip trees out of the ground? Lame Kansas wind! You tear the top off our car, throw my mom until she breaks her leg, make a car door cut my head open AND KILL MY SISTER, but you're too weak to fly a kite?"

He spun around and stomped back inside, dragging the kite behind him. His mom stepped silently out of the way as he slammed the front door and stomped back up the stairs. He stopped beside Willow's room. Frustration and anger bubbled to the surface. She should still be here. Why did she have to die? His familiar head rush and dizziness intensified. The tail of the kite fluttered. Brayden shook his head as he stuffed his feelings deep inside and slammed her door.

An alarm rang. Brayden jolted awake, breathing hard. Was that the tornado siren? He looked outside. The sun was just peeking over the rooftops. The trees weren't even swaying. He gazed around the room in confusion. The sound was coming from his clock. His alarm clock. He slammed it with his hand and the ringing stopped. It was Monday morning. Time to return to school.

The smell of bacon and eggs wafted upstairs. Leave it to Mom to encourage him with food. He threw on jeans and a green t-shirt, spiked his hair and sat at the kitchen table.

"Look at you, dressed and ready for the day," Mom said. She slid a mound of scrambled eggs on his plate, and then added two strips of sizzling bacon."

"Is this turkey bacon?" Brayden asked.

Mom shook her head. "No. I'll get back to being healthy later."

"Are you sure you don't want me to drive you to school?" asked Dad.

"No. I'll bike. You've been telling me to get exercise."

"True. Do you have all of your homework?" Dad continued.

"Yes." Brayden stuffed a fork full of eggs into his mouth.

"Is there anything else we can do for you?" Mom asked.

"No." He ate as quickly as possible. He didn't want to go to school, but he needed to get out of the house.

He slurped up the last of his orange juice and put his dishes in the sink. Banjo followed him, wagging his tail in expectation. Brayden scratched him behind his left ear and went upstairs to brush his teeth and grab his new backpack.

"I'll see you after school," he said reaching for the door to the garage.

"Wait," Mom called. She gave him a hug. "We love you."

Brayden nodded and walked out. He jammed his helmet on his head, causing him to immediately howl in pain. He pulled it back off, avoiding his bandage, and slammed the helmet onto the cement floor. The hard plastic shell cracked, reminding him of Willow's helmet.

Mom threw open the door and poked her head out. "Are you okay?"

"No. Does it matter?"

He pushed the bike onto the driveway and felt a sense of panic as the garage door rattled and wheezed shut. Time to face his school friends. He climbed on his bike and forced himself to continue down the street. His legs strained to pedal. It had been a long time since he had been on a bike, or had any exercise beyond a walk. He glanced behind him. The sidewalk was all wrong. No one was there to slow him down and embarrass him. No one struggled to catch up when he hit the button at the stop light. He smacked the light pole with his bare hand. This was all wrong. A breeze hit him in the face and he realized he was crying. He turned his bike around. Clearly, he wasn't ready for school. But what would he do at home? Stare at Willow's empty room? Hear another persuasive argument about school from his mom? There were no good options. He spun his bike back to the light pole. He had to keep going. Before he could change his mind, Brayden began to pedal. The brick façade of the high school loomed before him. He locked his bike at the school's stand and hesitantly walked through the front doors.

A sea of students parted to let him pass. He was used to that, but this time it was accompanied by stares and whispers. He gritted his teeth and kept walking until he reached his locker.

"Brayden!" Max yelled. "I was wondering when you'd be back."

"Here I am," he forced out.

"Hey, guys! Look who's here!" Max continued.

Trey, Parker, Gavin and Ian all strutted over and swarmed around their long lost friend.

"Hey! How's it going?" asked Ian.

Trey punched his arm. "What kind of dumb question is that? His sister just died. Get a clue."

Ian punched him back. "I was just making conversation."

"Cool stripe," Max said, pointing to Brayden's bandage.

"Is it true that a car door sliced your head in the tornado?" Gavin asked.

Brayden nodded.

"If you've got to get hurt, a tornado is a great way to do it," said Parker. "When people ask how you got your scar, you can tell them it's from a tornado. That sure beats something lame like falling off your bike."

"Yeah. I guess so," Brayden said.

"Too bad you didn't record it all on your phone or something," Ian commented. "Video from inside a tornado would be awesome. You probably could have made lots of money off it. You didn't record it, did you?"

"No, I was a little busy," Brayden muttered.

Trey punched Ian again. "I doubt if he wants a video since the tornado is what gave him his scar and killed his sister."

"And broke his mom's leg. Didn't I hear that the tornado broke her leg?" asked Gavin.

"Yeah. When she landed, our car crashed on her leg."

Ian's jaw dropped in amazement. "That is so—"

"Do I need to punch you again?" asked Trey.

"That is so awful," Ian said, punching Trey instead.

Brayden's head ached and he desperately wanted to stop talking about the tornado. "So, I guess we should actually go to class."

"Oh. Yeah. Class. We'll catch you later," said Max.

The guys wandered off to their own classrooms. Brayden grabbed his books and headed to World History.

The usual chatter stopped as soon as he stepped through the door.

"Welcome back, Brayden," Mr. Montoya said.

Brayden dropped his assignments from the last week into the wooden assignment box on the front desk. He avoided eye contact with his classmates as he walked to his seat.

"I'm assuming everyone did their reading last night," Mr. Montoya began, "so who can tell me the name of one of the greatest military leaders in history?"

No one raised their hand.

"He was also the emperor of France and conquered parts of Europe. Anyone know?"

Blank faces stared at him.

"Did anyone do their reading?" he shook his head. "A character in a movie with Pedro and Kip and Tina the llama was named after him."

Several hands shot up.

"Finally. Yes, Peyton?"

"Napoleon."

"Thank you. Yes, Napoleon Bonaparte. He was born in 1769 in Corsica. He went to a military school and was soon made the commander of the French Army in Italy where he..."

Brayden watched Mr. Montoya's mouth move, but his words seemed to slur together until everything he said sounded like gibberish. He thought back to the last time he sat in World History. The tornado hadn't happened. His head was uninjured. His sister was still alive. It seemed unreal to be back in this chair listening to facts about someone he really didn't care about long before he was ever alive. Why was he here?

Mr. Montoya was still talking. "Napoleon's invasion of Russia in 1812 resulted in a disastrous retreat. The tide started to turn in favor of the allies and in March 1814, Paris fell. Napoleon went into exile on the Mediterranean island of Elba."

Brayden caught a few more words. Going into exile sounded good. He really didn't want to be around people anymore. Not even his buddies. All of that talking just made his head pound. He didn't want people asking about the tornado. He just wanted to be left alone.

"The Battle of Waterloo ended his brief second reign," Mr. Montoya continued. "The British imprisoned him on the island of St. Helena, where he died on May 5th, 1821. Now, hopefully you took notes, but if not, you need to re-read chapter 14. Or, for many of you, read it for the first time. Remember that the final is coming up soon and this information will be on the test."

Brayden shook his head. How was he going to be able to concentrate enough for finals if he couldn't even focus through one class lecture? The bell rang and he followed his classmates out the door.

"Did you really get sucked up into a tornado?" asked a student he didn't even recognize.

"Yes." He kept walking.

"So, what was it like?" The student followed him.

"Windy." Brayden walked faster and ducked into another classroom.

Earth Science was a complete blur. He realized near the end of class that he had slept through most of it. His sleeve was wet from drool. He looked around the class to see if anyone had noticed. A few classmates gave him a weak pitying smile. Had he snored?

After class, he walked to the drinking fountain and splashed water on his face, trying to avoid his bandages. He was determined to stay awake in English. Trey and Max caught up with him.

"Were you hot?" asked Max.

"What?"

"Your face and hair are wet. Did you get hot?" Max repeated.

"Oh. No. I just can't stay awake."

"You're at school. What do you expect? I sleep through lots of my classes," said Trey.

They strolled into English together.

"Brayden. Good to see you again," said Mr. Hankenson. "Your Dad called to get your assignments last week. Were you able to get any done?"

"Yeah." Brayden handed his assignments to his teacher.

"Way to go." Mr. Hankenson grabbed a book off his desk. "We just started reading this last Friday. Try reading the first two chapters tonight if you can. Then you'll be caught up."

Brayden slumped into his seat. The book was called *The Hiding Place*. A picture of an old lady with glasses was on the cover. He sighed. Reading would be hard enough with an exciting book. This book looked like it would put him to sleep for sure. He rested his head on his arms and noticed marching soldiers on the cover next to the old lady. His eyebrows shot upwards. Maybe the book would at least be worth skimming. He rubbed the sides of his head, wishing his head would finally stop hurting.

"You need us to cheer you up," whispered Max. "I know what will help." He pulled a piece of paper from his notebook and wrote, "I survived the flood," on one side. He folded over one end and stuck it into Logan's collar.

Brayden didn't smile.

"Do you get it? His pants are always too short, and he wears those dorky white socks," Max clarified.

Brayden nodded, but just rested his head in his arms.

"Okay. How about this," said Trey. He wadded up a tiny piece of paper, stuck it into his mouth, and flicked it into Logan's hair. "You probably missed being part of the spitball brigade. Time to re-enlist. It might make you feel better."

"Maybe later," Brayden said.

Trey shrugged. He flicked two more spitballs into Logan's hair, but without an audience, he grew bored and put the paper away.

"What business did the ten Boom family run?" asked Mr. Hankenson.

Brayden was glad he would not be expected to know the answer. He debated on whether to rest or listen so he wouldn't have to read the first chapter.

"Kenzie?"

Brayden's head snapped up. She had completely slipped his mind. His head must have really been hit hard.

"They had a watch-repair business," she answered. Her eyes glanced in Brayden's direction.

He quickly looked straight ahead. No sense getting her mad at him again.

He attempted to listen to the rest of the questions about the book, but his mind wandered. Had Kenzie heard about his time in the hospital? Was she still mad at him for teasing Logan, and hanging out with his gang…and with just being who he was?

The bell rang. Brayden dropped his book and bent down to pick it up. The action caused his head to throb. He sat for a moment clutching his head until the pain eased.

"Are you okay?"

Brayden turned. It was Kenzie. "Yeah."

"I heard about all you've gone through. I can't even imagine how hard that would be."

"Yeah."

"If you need any help catching up in school or something, let me know."

"Uh...thanks."

She smiled at him and turned, bumping into Trey and Max. Her smile quickly morphed into a frown as she left the room.

"Wow. The Ice Queen is actually talking to you," Max commented.

"And it wasn't even a lecture," Trey added.

Brayden nodded. Maybe he could endure the rest of the day at school after all.

CHAPTER 14

WHIRLWIND

It was almost time to leave, but Brayden was still in bed staring at the ceiling.

Mom knocked on his door. "Brayden? I have breakfast on the table. Are you ready to go?"

"I'm not going to school today."

Mom leaned against the closed door and sighed. "And why is that?"

Brayden sat up. "Because I've been to school three days now, and people are still constantly asking me about the tornado and my head and Willow. I thought they would be over it by now, but it's like all the people who were too shy or polite to ask at first are starting to ask, and everyone who asked too many questions at first want to know more. I don't want to talk about it anymore."

"So what would you do if you stayed at home?"

"Enjoy some peace and quiet."

"And what? Count bumps on the ceiling? Play video games? You only have a week left. I need you to finish off the school year."

"But I can't concentrate. I try to listen, but I can't follow what the teachers are saying for more than five minutes. It's like my brain got scrambled in the tornado. I'm going to fail all of my finals."

"I'll talk to your teachers. Maybe they can give you modified tests, or grade them easier."

"Maybe."

"I need you to at least be in class, trying to learn. So get up. If you're not eating breakfast in five minutes I will be escorting you through the hallway to your first class. I'll be sure to drop a crutch at least once to draw more attention."

Brayden groaned, but he rolled out of bed and got dressed. He grumbled all of the way downstairs and picked at his warmed-up waffle.

"I knew you could do it," Mom said.

Dad patted Brayden's back. "Hang in there. One more week."

Brayden continued chewing.

"I have time to drop you off at school this morning, if you want a ride," Dad said.

"Yeah. That would help." Brayden shoveled in two more bites and grabbed his backpack.

"Are you going to do anything with your hair?" asked Mom.

Brayden jammed a Royals baseball cap on his head but tossed it aside when he felt his bandage. He ran his fingers through his hair instead and followed Dad out the door.

Traffic was backed-up in front of the school. Dad tapped on the steering wheel impatiently. They crept forward two feet and stopped again.

"You can just let me out here, if you want."

"That's okay. I'll get you a little closer."

They moved up two car spaces and stopped again. Dad shook his head. "How long does it take to get out of the car and close the door? You'd think they hadn't been doing it all year long."

"Dad, this is fine. Really."

"Maybe it will have to be. Have a good day."

"Even an average day would be an improvement," Brayden said. He ducked his head down, hoping no one would recognize him and start asking more questions.

"Is that you, Brayden?" someone called.

Brayden pretended not to hear and sprinted into the school building. He kept up the pace until he reached his locker.

Parker and Ian were standing five lockers down. They were holding a freshman boy upside down. A crowd gathered around them, snickering.

"What did you call me?" asked Parker.

"Nothing," the upside-down-kid stammered.

"I think you did. Maybe not to my face, but I heard it. Didn't you, Ian?"

"That I did."

"Tell us what you said," Parker commanded.

The freshman was turning red. "I said you were a brainless wonder who got his kicks out of terrorizing people."

"You're right about part of it," said Parker.

"What? That you're a brainless wonder?" the kid said. He flinched, prepared to be hit.

Parker and Ian shook him harder. His books fell out of his arms and slid across the floor.

"No. That I like terrorizing people like you. Should we bowl with him down the hall?"

Ian nodded. "I think we should."

125

The crowd cleared a bowling path. The guys spotted Brayden.

"Hey, Brayden," Parker called. "Do you want to help?"

"I'll pass."

Parker shrugged. "I guess your head is still too messed up. Your loss."

He and Ian swung the freshman backward and forward, finally sending him sliding down the hallway. The audience clapped and hooted as the kid curled into a ball, protecting his head as he slid. He smacked into a locker and sat dazed for a moment. The crowd continued laughing. The humiliated student gathered his books and stumbled the opposite direction.

Ian pounded Parker's back. "That was great!"

They walked to Brayden's locker, but he ignored them and hastened to class. His head was pounding and he was breathing hard. He didn't want to join in the congratulatory strutting. He wanted to punch them.

He scowled as he sat in his World History seat and had to concentrate on taking deep breaths. He could feel sweat beads form on his face.

"Brayden? Are you okay?" asked Mr. Montoya.

Brayden didn't answer. His head felt like he had been on a tilt-o-whirl ride five times in a row. He stared at the papers on his desk, trying to calm down. One blew onto the floor. Or did he knock it off? He clutched the sides of his desk, trying to stuff his feelings inside where he could manage them.

"Brayden?"

He looked up. The rest of the class was staring at him. He closed his eyes and took another deep breath. His heart rate slowed down enough that he could and loosen his grip on the desk.

"Do you need to go to the nurse?" asked Mr. Montoya.

Brayden shook his head and slid down in his seat. His teacher studied him for a moment and then began the review for the final. Brayden bent down to pick up the paper at his feet. He pulled a blue pen from his notebook and attempted to take notes, certain he needed this information to get through the test. Soon scenes from World History were replaced with scenes from recent history, like the tornado, time with Willow, and the episode in the hallway. He shook his head. It was hopeless.

In Earth Science, he was relieved when the teacher passed out study guides. No blanks to fill in. No notes to take. Perfect. Maybe he could actually pass this class.

He skimmed through the guide. There was information on sheet erosion, plate boundaries, stress faults, earthquakes, volcanoes...Why wasn't there anything on tornadoes? Would more knowledge about tornadoes have kept his family safe? He began to replay the entire episode in his mind.

"Brayden?"

He looked up. "Yes?"

His teacher cocked his head to the side. "The bell rang."

Brayden looked around. Most of the class had already left. His face flushed as he quickly gathered his books. At least the day wasn't dragging by as much as usual. He shuffled into the hallway.

"There he is!" said a girl with long, brown hair.

Four girls flocked around Brayden. He kept walking.

"My little sister was friends with Willow," one of the girls said. "She cried when she heard that Willow died. She wanted to go to the funeral, but I had a track meet, so Mom said she couldn't go. Were there lots of people there?"

Brayden nodded.

"I heard some of her friends played clarinet at the funeral. I have to admit, I was surprised, because I know how awful my sister sounds on her flute. Of course, this is the first year they played. I bet that was hard listening to, huh?"

Brayden shook his head. His head started to pound again. Why wouldn't they go away?

"What did—"

Kenzie swooped in and grabbed Brayden's arm. "Sorry, girls. I need help with my homework and class is about to start." She pulled him away from the mob and escorted him down the hall.

The pounding in his head faded away. "Thanks," he said.

"No problem. Some people don't have a clue."

"Seems that way."

"I just finished reading our book last night. You know, *The Hiding Place*. Were you able to read it?" she asked.

"Actually, I'm almost done with it. It's one of the few things I've been able to focus on. It's a lot better than I thought it would be."

A tall senior with a nose piercing stopped short when he saw them. "Hey! Aren't you the tornado kid? What was it like to be inside one?"

"I am so sorry," Kenzie interrupted. "We're trying to get to English early to cram for finals. Maybe he'll catch you later."

They ducked into class before he could reply.

"I think *you* need a hiding place," Kenzie said.

"Maybe that's why I like the book." Brayden actually smiled. Such a strange feeling.

Mr. Hankenson was watching the clock. The bell rang and he cleared his throat. "We have lots to cram into these last few days. We'll finish discussing *The Hiding Place*

128

today, and then start reviewing for our final tomorrow. So, let's get right to it. On the night the Nazis invaded Holland, Corrie had a vision. What did she see?"

Brayden was shocked that he actually knew the answer. Was the fog finally lifting? He was tempted to raise his hand, but before he could act, Logan had answered the question. Brayden stayed focused through three more questions. He glanced at Kenzie. She smiled at him.

"Why was Corrie thrown into solitary confinement at Scheveningen Prison?" Mr. Hankenson asked.

Solitary confinement did not sound bad right now, at least, not if the confinement could be in the comfort of his own home. He wouldn't want the type of solitary confinement Corrie had, but being alone sounded good. No one to ask him questions about the tornado. Not having to watch his friends intimidate underclassmen. He'd like to just play his video games and sleep. Of course, reading a book might not be bad if it was as good as *The Hiding Place*. And seeing a few people would be okay. Like his Mom and Dad, as long as they weren't nagging him. Or Kenzie. Yeah. She was actually really nice now that she didn't seem to hate him.

Max flicked him on the shoulder. "Are you awake up there?"

"What?"

"Can you pass back the study guides? Look in front of you."

A stack of study guides were perched precariously on the edge of his desk. He grabbed them, but three still managed to fall to the floor. He scooped them up and passed them back.

"Where did you go?" Max asked. "La la land?"

"Yeah. I guess so."

"No worries. I frequent there myself."

Brayden stole a glance at Kenzie. She had a concerned look on her face.

The bell rang. Brayden took his time gathering his books, hoping that maybe Kenzie would want to talk. She was busy talking to Mr. Hankenson at the front of the class. He shrugged and walked out the door with Max and Trey.

By Algebra II, Brayden's brief moment of clarity had passed. Mrs. Brinkhaus started reviewing problems involving logarithms and exponents. It seemed to blow right over his head. He had never been an outstanding student. He felt good if his report card hung out in the B range. Unfortunately, he sensed disaster on the horizon. It seemed impossible for him to focus on a class for more than fifteen minutes. How was he supposed to concentrate enough to take a final for two hours?

He watched the students around him. They were actually paying attention and taking notes. He looked at the problem Mrs. Brinkhaus showed on the screen.

"So, what is the sum of the infinite geometric series $1/2 + 1/4 + 1/8 + 1/16...$"

Brayden shook his head. Nevermind. Even with a clear head he would probably be lost. He wondered if his mom had talked to the teachers about finals week. It was embarrassing having her call the school, but maybe it would help.

The bell rang. Kenzie walked up to the teacher's desk again. She was taking finals even more seriously than he expected. So much for talking to her. Of course, did he really think that they were that close just because she had helped him out and talked to him a few times? He needed to face reality and move on.

CHAPTER 15

THUNDER RUMBLE

By the time Brayden arrived at the lunch table, Parker and Ian were already enacting their freshman bowling story. Max, Trey and Gavin were all laughing.

"Did you hear about this?" Max asked Brayden.

"Hear about it!" Parker exclaimed. "He *saw* it."

"I wish I had been there," said Trey.

"Brayden didn't seem to enjoy it as much as everybody else," Ian stated.

"Oh, yeah? Why not, Brayden?" Max asked.

"He doesn't seem to enjoy anything yet," Ian answered for him. "That tornado really threw him off."

Max punched Ian's arm. "Being in a murdering tornado would throw anyone off."

"Yeah. But for how long?" asked Ian.

"I wish I knew," Brayden answered. He pulled a ham sandwich out of his lunch sack, but discovered his appetite was gone. His friends had already devoured most of their food. He tossed the sandwich on the center of the table with all of the empty wrappers. Ian, Parker, and Gavin tore into it like a pack of starving hyenas.

Kenzie and two of her friends suddenly veered towards their table. The guys looked at each other in surprise. Gavin's share of the sandwich dropped out of his open mouth.

"Sorry to interrupt you pouncing on food and what I'm sure was an amazing conversation, but I need to talk to Brayden for a second," Kenzie said.

Gavin stuffed the chunk of food back into his mouth.

"Go ahead," said Parker.

Kenzie rolled her eyes and turned to Brayden. "Can I talk to you alone?"

The guys started whistling cat calls.

"Girls, can you keep these animals at bay for a minute?"

"We'll try," Lindsay answered.

Brayden got up so quickly his chair tipped over. He followed Kenzie around the corner.

"Sorry. I had to get you away from your...friends," she said. "I didn't want them to overhear us."

"Overhear what?" asked Brayden.

"I noticed you were having a hard time paying attention in English and Algebra II lately."

Brayden hung his head. "Obvious, huh? Is everyone else noticing?"

"I don't know about everyone. Most of them are pretty self-absorbed, especially at this time of year. Either way, it's nothing to be embarrassed about. You've been through more than any of us. The point is, I figured you weren't able to take very good notes to get ready for finals."

"Not really."

"So I was thinking, it might help if you had a copy of my notes. I didn't want the teachers to think we were cheating

132

so--please don't get mad--I asked Mr. Hankenson and Mrs. Brinkhaus if they could make a copy of my notes to give to you."

Brayden's jaw dropped. "That's what you were doing after their classes today?"

Kenzie nodded. "If I'm interfering too much, I'm sorry. I just want to help."

"No. That's great. I mean, I didn't know how I was going to pass any finals…except maybe in science…because we got a completed study guide," he rambled. "That would help a lot."

She smiled and pulled the copies out of her folder. Brayden tried not to stare at her. She had to be one of the prettiest girls at the school. Especially now that she didn't think he was pond scum.

"Thanks. I really appreciate this."

"You bet." She turned toward the guys and shook her head. "I probably should rescue my friends from your friends. The poor girls can only stand so much."

Brayden walked back to the lunch table with her. The guys started whistling again.

"Oh, good," said Lindsay. "We were afraid our IQ was going to drop if we had to stay here much longer."

"Yeah? Well we were afraid that..." Parker paused, trying to think of a good comeback.

"We were afraid we'd need glasses to repair our vision after seeing all of you up too close," Max finished for him.

"That's possible. Our beauty can be blinding," said Marissa.

The girls laughed and walked away.

"What did she want?" asked Trey.
Brayden folded the notes in half. "She just wanted to give me some stuff from class."

"Are you working the sympathy angle with her?" asked Gavin. "'Cuz it seems to be working."

"Maybe I should get sucked up into a tornado, so I can get girls chasing me," said Ian.

Trey and Max both punched him in the arm.

"What?!"

"It'd take more than a tornado to make girls come after you," said Gavin.

Brayden actually smiled. Was that twice in one day? The guys split up at their lockers and headed to class. Brayden was almost to Spanish when two guys stopped him. One was so tall he stooped down to talk.

"John and Sid here. But you probably knew that. We're finishing up the yearbook. Yes, I know. We missed our deadline, so you'll get your yearbook at the beginning of next year. Anyhow, we have a couple pages to fill and would like to tell your story. We just have a few questions for you. Like what did it sound like in the tornado?"

"Loud."

"Can you elaborate? That won't help our word count very much," Sid said.

"Very loud."

John sighed. "How many stitches did you get after the car door slammed into your head?"

"Forty-seven."

"Does it still hurt?" Sid asked.

"Yes."

"What was it like to feel your sister ripped from your hands?" John asked.

Brayden scowled. The pounding began in his head again. "I have to get to class." He turned and started walking quickly down the hall.

"Wait! We have more questions!" Sid called.

Brayden grabbed his head. The hallway started to tilt back and forth like he was in a rocking chair. He stumbled to the Spanish room and fell into his seat. Just when he thought he might be able to make it through the last week of school. Why couldn't people leave him alone? He closed his eyes, waiting for the dizziness to subside.

Mrs. Hernandez bent down beside his desk. "Do you need to go to the nurse?"

Brayden squinted at her. "I think I'll be okay once the room stops spinning. It usually doesn't last long now."

"If you need anything, let me know."

"Thanks."

It was midway through the class before Brayden felt like he could take notes. He sighed. Too bad Kenzie wasn't in this class so she could help him catch up for finals. His head was just not cooperating. Two more classes left in the day. And then another week. It was just too much.

He managed to avoid talking to anyone on his way to PE. The locker room smelled like sweat and feet, so he quickly changed into his gym clothes and joined his class.

"Sorry, Brayden," said Mr. Williams, looking over his clip board. He adjusted the whistle hanging around his neck. "We're playing dodge ball today and we can't risk you getting hit in the head. I'll still give you participation points, but you need to just sit on the sidelines--far away from the balls."

Brayden nodded and sat under the electronic scoreboard. Dodge ball was a great diversion. Balls were soon flying all over the gym. He watched for a few minutes, but soon sprawled out and fell asleep.

Gavin nudged him. "We're done. You might want to get dressed before your last class."

"Yeah. Thanks," he said, stretching. He hadn't even broken a sweat, so he avoided the showers, making it easily to computer class before the bell rang.

The computer assignment was written on the white board. Brayden's head was clearer than usual thanks to his nap, so he decided to get started right away. He was so absorbed in his work, that he didn't hear Max drop into the seat beside him.

"Hey, what's the rush?" Max asked.

"My head isn't hurting, so I'm working while I can."

"That's gotta stink--not knowing when you're going to get dizzy and all. Maybe you'll be back to normal next week."

"Yeah." Brayden kept working.

Max followed his example and started his assignment, too. The clicking of their fingers on the keys replaced their usual comments to classmates.

Ms. Snell walked by their computers. "Wow, guys. This is a switch. Keep it up."

"Aye, aye, captain," Max said, pausing to salute.

Ms. Snell paused and then continued walking down the row, shaking her head. When she reached the corner she stopped again. Two girls were deep in conversation and were oblivious to her presence.

"While your discussion is very interesting, and I want to hear what Grant told you after lunch, I need you to get started on your assignment. You can talk more after you're done."

Some of the guys laughed. The two girls blushed and turned their chairs toward their computers. Ms. Snell resumed walking the aisles, checking on her students' progress.

Thunder rumbled, causing several students to jump in their seats. The lights blinked. Brayden felt his heart rate accelerate.

"Did anyone lose data?" asked Ms. Snell. "Any power issues?"

Everyone shook their head. Chatter erupted in various parts of the room.

"Good. Back to work."

The thunder continued to rumble occasionally. There were no windows in the classroom, so the class could only *hear* the storm. Rain started to pelt the roof. Brayden stopped typing. His hands began to sweat and he wiped them on his jeans.

"You okay?" asked Max.

Brayden tried to smile, but it looked more like a grimace. "Yeah. I'm good."

He tightened his jaw, intent on remaining calm through the rain and thunder. With hunched shoulders, he started typing again. The uneasiness grew inside of him, but he was determined to have one class where he completed an assignment. More thunder. Or was that the pounding in his head? He rubbed his temples, trying to ease the growing pain.

Ms. Snell stood behind him. "Take a break, Brayden. I'm afraid you might hyperventilate."

"I'm almost done."

He continued working, battling the storm that was inside him. Just one class. One class where he didn't feel like a complete loser. Sweat oozed out and dripped down his forehead. He wiped his eyes.

"Are you sweating or crying?" asked Max.

Brayden looked up and felt his head. "Sweating."

"Relax. It isn't that big of a deal."

But to Brayden it was. He kept working. The computer screen looked like it was tipping to the left. He closed his eyes and finished the sentence.

"Let's call that good enough," Ms. Snell said, placing a hand on his shoulder. "I appreciate your determination, but you look like you're about to explode. Do you think you can walk?"

Brayden opened his eyes. The computer was upright again. He nodded.

"Good. The bell's going to ring in a few minutes. Why don't you get a head start to your locker?"

"Bye, Brayden," said Max.

"Later," he answered. He grabbed his notebook and tried to ignore all the eyes staring at him as he escaped through the door. He staggered to his locker as quickly as his head would allow, grabbed his backpack and headed to the main door.

His phone buzzed. There was a text from his mom. She would be driving because it was raining hard. Relief washed over him. The quicker he got home the better. The bell rang just as he walked out the front door. Mom blinked the headlights to a car he didn't recognize and he dashed inside. She was the first in a long line of vehicles.

"How are you?" she asked.

"Wet."

She nodded, started the car and pulled out onto the main street.

"Whose car?" he asked.

"Ours now. The insurance check from the totaled car came last week. Dad decided it was time to replace the Camry. This car is several years old, but didn't have many miles on it."

"I'm glad some things are replaceable."

The windshield wipers frantically swept water to the sides of the glass. The skies were gray and dreary. Brayden shook his head, spraying water all over the dashboard. Mom always teased him when he did that, saying he and Banjo were like brothers. He looked over at her, waiting for her comment.

It was obvious she had not even noticed his dog-like shake. She was staring intently out the windshield, gripping the steering wheel so hard her knuckles protruded. Her face was pale and her cheeks glistened. Was it from the rain, or was she crying?

"Mom, are you okay?" he asked.

She kept her face forward. "This is harder than I thought it would be. I just need to get you home."

"Is it hard because you broke your leg?"

"No. This car's an automatic, so I don't have to use my bad leg. I…Driving during a storm brings up too many memories."

Brayden squeezed his mom's shoulder. Evidently, he was not the only one who had storm issues.

CHAPTER 16

DANCE IN THE RAIN

When Brayden came downstairs the next morning, he was surprised to find Dad in the kitchen, pouring two glasses of grape juice.

"Do you want flakes or granola or what?" Dad asked. He yawned and stroked his chin, finding a patch of stubble he missed while shaving.

"I can pour my own cereal. Where's Mom?"

"The storm kept her awake all night. She and Banjo were in the basement until about 5:00 this morning. I didn't want to wake her up."

Brayden nodded and poured a bowl of cornflakes. He sloshed milk over it, grabbed his juice, and sat at the table. Dad joined him.

"So, you've almost made it through your first week back to school. How's it going?"

"Hasn't Mom been telling you? I can't seem to get through a single class without zoning out, having a dizzy spell or a raging headache. It's a waste of time."

"I know Mom called the school. Maybe they'll work something out for you," Dad said.

"Maybe."

"Hang in there. Only six more days."

Brayden slurped up the last few bites of cereal. "That seems like a very long time right now."

"I suppose it does. Do you want a ride to school?"

"No. That's okay. I don't want Mom to have to pick me up." Brayden grabbed his backpack.

"Wait. Bowl in the sink."

Brayden rolled his eyes but did as he was told. "Bye, Dad."

"Hope your day goes better."

"Me, too."

Brayden flung his backpack on and pedaled to school. His day was thrown off. Mom was always there in the mornings. Of course, so was Willow—until the tornado. He pedaled faster to distract his mind. He didn't want head trouble right from the beginning.

He zipped past three girls taking their time walking in the center of the sidewalk.

"Hey! Watch it!" the blond snapped.

One of her friends grabbed her arm. "Wait. That's the tornado boy. Ease up."

Brayden swerved to avoid the fire hydrant. *The tornado boy*? He shook his head. This year could not end soon enough. He locked his bike at the rack, waited for a mob to pass him, and then slipped inside.

He was relieved to see the guys weren't at his locker and that there were no human bowling scenes in the hallway. Sid and John spotted him and rushed toward his locker, waving their notebooks and pencils.

"Remember us? From the yearbook," Sid called. "Are you in the mood now to answer some questions?"

Brayden escaped into his World History class and sat immediately in his seat. John stuck his head inside, but Brayden pretended to be busy looking through his notes. The bell rang and John's head disappeared.

"All right, class," Mr. Montoya began. "The day you've all been waiting for. The last day of regular history class has finally arrived."

The students started cheering. Brayden winced at the noise.

"Okay. Simmer down. We'll finish our review and then you'll be all set for finals. This will be your first test of the week, so come bright and early on Monday morning, turn in your book and then get started. Make sure to bring a sharpened pencil and don't be late."

The intercom buzzed. "Mr. Montoya?"

"Yes?"

"Can you please send Brayden Kesler to the office?"

"Certainly." Mr. Montoya smiled at Brayden. "You've been freed. See you soon."

Brayden gathered his books and slipped out the door. Fortunately, Sid and John were not waiting for him. He entered the office and stood in front of the reception desk.

The secretary smiled at him and then sneezed. She grabbed a tissue and dabbed at her red nose. "Allergies. I love them. Good to see you, Brayden. I'm so sorry to hear about your sister. You can go on into the counselor's room. She wanted to meet with you."

She sneezed again as he walked past the nurse's office and the teacher's workroom. He hesitated before knocking on Mrs. Patel's door.

"Come on in, Brayden," she said.

He couldn't remember being in her office before. He sat on a purple microfiber chair, and started reading the posters on her wall. A picture of a square present in purple and green polka-dotted wrapping paper said, "Yesterday is history, tomorrow is a mystery. Today is a gift, that's why we call it the present." He'd heard that one before.

Another poster showed an unusual looking cartoon kid and said, "Be yourself, everyone else is already taken." Not bad.

The next picture had a mountain scene with a path winding through it. It said, "Your future is created by what you do today, not tomorrow."

He was beginning to feel overwhelmed by all the witty massages, but turned to read the poster behind him. A cloudy sky surrounded a girl with an umbrella and rain boots. It said, "Don't wait for a storm to pass, learn how to dance in the rain." He peered closer at the little girl. She had blond, wispy hair just like Willow. His stomach twisted.

Mrs. Patel twirled in her spinning chair until she faced him. She was wearing a traditional sari from India and had her long, black hair in a twist at the back of her head. "It's good to see you. We were all obviously very concerned about you when we heard about your tangle with the tornado. I was impressed that you came to school every day this week. I'm sure that wasn't easy."

Brayden shook his head.

"Your mom called yesterday and said she was worried about how you would fare during finals week. She said you have a hard time concentrating? Is that right?"

Brayden nodded.

"Is that because of the physical trauma to your head or because of the emotional trauma from losing your sister?"

"Both."

"Very understandable. I talked to each of your teachers yesterday. They all noticed how challenging this is for you, and want to work with you to come up with a solution for finals week. We have a suggestion, and you can tell me what you think."

"Okay."

"They would like you to go to each final like everyone else and get as far as you can on each test. When class is over, turn it in like your classmates."

"Okay?" Brayden was confused. That didn't sound helpful at all.

"But then at the end of the day, stop by my office. I will give the test back to you to take home. You can take your time finishing it and can even check it with your notes if that helps. Then, as soon as you arrive to school the next day, hand the test back to me and I will return it to your teacher. That way, you aren't embarrassed and your classmates don't get angry thinking we're being unfair. They don't need to know that we're making special allowances for you. Would that relieve your pressure?"

Brayden's eyes were wide. "Yes."

"Are there any changes you would like to make?"

"No. That sounds great."

She smiled. "Good. Now I've also been told about your dizzy spells and intense head pain. Are these constant, or do they seem to be triggered by something?"

"Right after the...right afterwards, my head always hurt, and the dizziness was...I guess it was most of the time. Now I still have a constant dull ache and the stitches are starting to itch, but sometimes my head starts pounding and I get so dizzy I can hardly stand it."

"Does that happen at certain times of the day or does something happen right before it?"

Brayden thought for a moment. "It usually gets the worst when I think about the tornado. Or Willow. I still think about it a lot on my own, but I try to think about my school work or something... anything else. It seems like everyone I bump into wants to talk about it or ask questions about it." He looked at Mrs. Patel and his face reddened. "No offense, I know that's your job...but for everyone else it's like they're just curious, or trying to be nice, but it's annoying. I don't want to think about it. I thought that it would get better after the first day or two of school, but people still bring it up all of the time."

"I can see how that would be hard. School should be a good distraction, but instead, the other students keep forcing you to think about it again. Is that right?"

"Yes."

"So, what happens when you start thinking about the tornado and Willow?"

"My head starts pounding and my heart beats faster. I feel like I want to explode. I try to calm down and look normal so everyone doesn't think I'm a freak. I stuff it in and then I feel dizzy and sick to my stomach."

"So stuffing it in makes it worse?"

"I guess so. But I don't have a choice. I can't start throwing things or running around in the middle of class."

"And that's what you feel like doing?"

"Yes. And yelling. And breaking things or...punching something."

"That's a lot to try to hold in."

"Yeah."

"But you're right--that wouldn't go over very well in class."

"No."

"So you stuffing it in is painful, but you can't let it out--at least not in the way you want."

"Right."

Mrs. Patel sat for a moment, tapping her pencil against her cheek. She spun back around to her desk and pulled a black notebook out of a drawer. She turned to face him again. "In the classroom we're a bit limited, especially during finals week. I know this sounds a bit silly, but I want you to give it a try. When you first start feeling the storm inside you, I want you to pull out this notebook and start writing how you feel. Try to focus all your frustration and pain through the pencil and onto the paper. You can be very subtle about it. Students may see you writing, but they'll think you're working on your final. Keep writing until you start feeling better."

"But what if that doesn't work?" asked Brayden. "I'm not much of a writer. That was Willow's thing."

"Just give it a try, and tell me how it goes. If we need to come up with something else, we will."

Brayden nodded.

"Stop by any time. Just tell your teacher you need to go to the office. I'll let them know that it's to see me."

"Even in the middle of a final?"

"If it gets really uncontrollable. Otherwise try to wait until you're between classes."

Brayden took a deep breath. He felt like a stone was lifting off his chest. "Thanks."

"Not a problem." Mrs. Patel scribbled out a pass and handed it to him on top of the black notebook. She looked at the clock. "You'll want to head to your second-hour class. We had a lot to talk about."

146

He looked at the poster with the girl that reminded him of Willow. He certainly wasn't ready to dance in the rain, but maybe it was now possible to endure the storm.

CHAPTER 17

CLOSET BREEZE

Sunlight peeked through Brayden's blinds, casting bright lines on his navy comforter. After two days of intermittent rain and blustering wind, the sun was a welcome sight. He rubbed his eyes, grateful for a chance to sleep in and for a day without school. Banjo nosed the door open and jumped on his bed.

"Hey, boy."

Banjo licked his face. HIs breath smelled like dog food and stale cheese. He sat on Brayden's chest, wagging his tail.

"Are you trying to get me out of bed?"

Banjo licked his face again. Brayden stretched and staggered down the stairs, not even bothering to change out of his striped pajama pants and old t-shirt.

"Welcome to the land of the living," said Dad.

"You must have been tired," Mom added. "It's already 10:30."

"Really? Sorry."

"Don't be," she said. "Sleep is good for you. I should take lessons, because I can't seem to sleep for more than a few hours at a time. We had pancakes. Would you like me to warm some up for you?"

"That sounds good. Three, please."

Mom placed the pancakes on a plate and stuck them in the microwave. "Jam or syrup?"

"Syrup."

The microwave beeped repeatedly until she pulled out the pancakes and syrup and placed them in front of Brayden. He took a huge bite.

"Did you have anything you wanted to do today?" asked Mom.

Brayden finished chewing. "Not really." He crammed in more food.

She sat at the kitchen table and looked down at her hands. "I thought I might start sorting through some of Willow's clothes to give to charity."

Brayden choked on his pancake and had to drink a long sip of apple juice. "Already? What's the rush?"

"There isn't a rush. I just...can't seem to get any closure. I walk into her room and still feel like she's just away at a friend's house. I look in her closet and wonder why it's so clean. She usually had clothes piled on the floor. Kind of like you do. It's like I can't seem to accept she's gone."

"So you want to just move on and wipe away any trace of her?" Brayden asked with an edge to his voice.

Dad raised an eyebrow. "Careful, Brayden."

"Not at all," Mom answered. Her lips quivered. "My doctor just thinks I won't start to heal until I can accept that she's not coming back."

"Maybe your doctor should run his ideas past Nurse Fonda first. He's probably never had a family member die. Fonda understands. She could give you better advice."

149

"I'm not talking about the doctor who operated on my leg. I'm talking about my new doctor. He's more of a grief counselor," Mom clarified.

"Has he ever had a sister or daughter die?"

"I don't know. I didn't ask."

"Maybe you should. I don't think we should give Willow's stuff away. I think we should just leave her room the way it is."

"We didn't plan on giving *everything* away," Dad said. "We just thought we'd donate her clothes."

"So was that supposed to be part of a fun family day together? Count me out. She's only been gone a few weeks!" Brayden shoved his chair back. It toppled to the floor. He stomped up the stairs, leaving the rest of his pancakes untouched.

The door to Willow's room was closed. Brayden flung it open. How could they ever remove her stuff? He sat on her bed with the purple comforter and rainbow pillows. He fingered the shaggy pink and purple striped blanket at the foot of the bed. She liked to drape the blanket over her head and shoulders and sneak up on people, banging into walls on the way. It used to be annoying, but now he'd do anything to have her do it again.

Her drawings were taped all over the walls. Most of them were cartoon animals. One picture vaguely resembled his family, except in dog form. He looked closer. The french poodle wore a necklace and flowered dress, a great dane had reading glasses and a tie, a bulldog had gelled hair and wore his favorite shirt, and a white maltese had a bow in her hair and a pencil in her mouth.

Stuffed animals were still scattered all over the room. He picked up a stuffed pig and squeezed it. There was no way they could just give all of this away. They could never turn

150

this room into a sterile office or guest bedroom. This would always be Willow's room--at least to him. He dropped the pig and pulled the closet door open. Her clothes hung neatly, just like his mom said. She couldn't get rid of them. At least not today. He felt the familiar spinning start in his head, and had to lean against the closet door. The clothes rippled as if a gentle breeze blew through the closet.

Brayden shook his head. "I don't believe in ghosts," he said out loud. "I was joking when my pesky cousins were here."

The clothes swayed harder. His heart began to beat faster and he started to back up.

A hand touched his shoulder. He yelped and spun around.

"Oh. Sorry," Dad said. "I was just going to talk to you."

"Did you see the clothes move?"

Dad looked in the closet. The clothes were still. "No. Did you?"

"Yes." Brayden stared into the closet, waiting for more movement. Nothing.

"Maybe you need to go back to bed. We don't have to go anywhere. You probably had to push yourself too hard this week." He tried to guide him out of the room.

Brayden pulled away. "I'm not going crazy. The clothes were blowing around."

"Maybe the air conditioner came on for a few minutes."

"The vent is on the other side of the room."

Dad sighed. "Can we just go into your room and talk?"

"Why can't we talk here? Does this room make you feel uncomfortable--especially knowing you are about to pack everything away?" Brayden stubbornly sat back down on Willow's bed and crossed his arms.

"We aren't going to pack everything away. We just wanted to give the clothes away."

"Do you honestly think someone is going to want to wear clothes belonging to a dead person?" Brayden asked. "Here, Cousin Susie. Enjoy wearing Willow's dress. She's dead, but maybe you'll manage to live past eleven."

Dad's jaw twitched. "We were going to give the clothes to needy kids. They wouldn't need to know they belonged to someone who died. It's not like Willow had a disease and they could catch it. She didn't infect the clothes. She didn't die wearing any of these clothes."

"I know that all too well," Brayden said. His anger started to dissolve into sadness. "I can still picture her purple *Shine On* t-shirt whipping in the wind when I was trying to hold onto her legs." A lump grew in his throat. "I remember the same shirt in ribbons when they covered her with a gray wool blanket."

Dad sat on the bed beside him. "I remember that too. I think the image will be stuck in my mind forever."

"Then why are you and Mom in such a hurry to clear things out and forget?"

"We don't want to forget. We just want to start healing. The doctor thought giving the clothes away would help. That's all we were going to do."

"Can it wait a little longer?" Brayden asked. "I'm just not ready."

"It can wait." Dad put his arm around Brayden's shoulders. "At some point I think we'll need to give them away. But not today."

Brayden breathed easier. "Thanks, Dad."

"You're welcome." He stood up. "Now, don't you have finals next week? You should probably be studying."

"I guess it wouldn't hurt to look over my study guides and notes." He followed Dad out of Willow's room, but paused and turned. "I did see her clothes move."

"If you say so. Maybe you should take a nap before you study." Dad looked into his son's eyes. "Concussions can do strange things to your head."

"Yeah." Brayden walked into his room and shut the door. He knew his head wasn't reliable right now, but he was convinced that he saw movement.

His green backpack was jammed in his closet, where he had tossed it last night. He unzipped it and pulled out his folder filled with study guides and notes. The black notebook from the school counselor poked out of the backpack. He stared at it. Maybe he should start writing how he was feeling today. He pulled it out and flipped to the first blank page, but he didn't know what to write. Writing was Willow's thing, not his. He closed the notebook and crammed it into the backpack. Maybe he would try again at school.

Banjo huffed outside Brayden's door.

"You want in?" Brayden asked.

Banjo whined in return, so Brayden swung the door open.

The beagle waddled in. His stomach was swollen and almost drug on the floor. He flopped at Brayden's feet and emitted a fowl, yeasty burp.

"What's wrong with you?"

Banjo rolled over onto his back. Brayden scratched the exposed, rounded belly but his dog didn't wag his tail. He whined instead.

Mom hollered from the kitchen. "Did either of you do something with the loaf of bread I just baked? I had it cooling on the counter and now it's gone."

Brayden looked at his dog. Banjo whined and burped again.

"Was Banjo in the kitchen while it was cooling?" he asked.

"I don't know. Why?"

"Come see for yourself."

Mom hobbled upstairs and peeked in the door. Banjo gave a pathetic whine in greeting, but did not get to his feet. She bent down for a closer look. Brayden noticed that her eyes were red and swollen.

"There are bread crumbs in his whiskers!" she exclaimed.

Banjo licked his chops removing the evidence. He struggled to get back to his feet and waddled to the door.

"That bread was made entirely out of whole wheat flour," Mom said. "That's too much fiber for a dog. I'm keeping him in the backyard in case he explodes. Crazy thing." She turned to leave.

"Hey, Mom?" Brayden said.

She turned back around.

"I'm sorry if I made you cry."

She nodded.

"I can't seem to figure out how to handle Willow being gone," he admitted.

"I can't either." She rubbed her neck. "I want to make it easier for you...for all of us...but nothing seems to help. That's why I went to a doctor--or I guess you could call him a psychiatrist—but that just makes me feel...incompetent. Let's call him a counselor." She rubbed her forehead. "I should be able to handle mental issues."

"I saw the school counselor today. I guess that's almost the same thing. I felt like a loser walking in, but I think she's going to be a big help. She told me to work on finals in class and then pick up the tests after school if I need more time to finish them."

"Sounds like a good plan," Mom said.

"Yeah. Thanks for talking to her."

"Sure. I'm glad I did something right. It looks like I'll need you to be patient with me while I stumble through everything else. I *am* trying," she said.

"I know."

They heard a heaving sound outside the door.

"Oh, no!" Mom scrambled toward the sound. "Banjo!"

"Did he explode?" asked Brayden.

"Yes. All over the hallway carpet. Lovely," Mom complained. "Come on, Banjo. You are going outside!"

"Do you need help cleaning?" asked Brayden. "It's probably hard for you to scrub the floor with your bad leg."

"Really?" Mom asked. "You're volunteering?"

"Well, not exactly. I was going to ask Dad to do it. Dad!" Brayden yelled. "Mom needs help cleaning!"

The smell of vomit swirled down the hallway. Brayden closed his door and opened his bedroom window. He grabbed his study guides and began reading. A few minutes later he turned on the ceiling fan to diffuse the stench. He could hear his dad grumbling over the noise from the steam cleaner. He grinned and returned to his bed. Even studying was better than cleaning up after a sick dog. He didn't know how long his head would cooperate, but he was motivated to try.

CHAPTER 18

WINDS OF CHANGE

Monday morning came all too soon. Brayden ate his fill of eggs, bacon, and toast (made from a new loaf of homemade bread that cooled on the *inner* burner of the stove, out of Banjo's reach). He biked slowly to school, dreading a week filled with tests, and joined the mob of students flooding the high school.

Max pushed his way through the crowd until he caught up with Brayden. "Are you ready for this?"

"I guess I have to be," said Brayden. "How about you?"

"Good enough." He looked at Brayden's bandage-free forehead. "Cool stitches. How's the head?"

"A little better."

Parker ran up behind them and smacked Max in the head. "Hey, guys," he said.

"How's *your* head?" asked Brayden.

"Sore now." Max smacked Parker back.

They each separated into their first hour finals.

Mr. Montoya was standing at the classroom door. "Place your World History books in a stack on the front table and then find your seats," he instructed.

By the time Brayden made it to the front table, there was already a teetering tower of books. He carefully set his on top, hoping he wouldn't send the whole stack crashing down. The stack swayed, but stayed upright. He found his seat.

After three more people, the tower collapsed. A few students returned to restack the books.

Mr. Montoya shook his head. "Try stacking them in more than one tower," he suggested.

Once all of the books were restacked and the students were seated, Mr. Montoya grabbed a pile of tests. "Clear your desks of everything but a pencil. There is to be no talking or getting up. Once you receive your test, you may begin."

Brayden shoved his black notebook under his desk. Evidently, the journaling idea would not work for every class. He hoped he didn't need it.

Mr. Montoya placed a test on his desk and smiled. "You can do this."

Brayden nodded and looked over the test. He was relieved to discover that the first section was multiple choice. There were questions about social classes, Louis the XVI, and the Berlin Conference. He skimmed through the choices and was pleased to be able to choose answers he felt confident in.

The next section was matching. It was a little harder, but he was able to make educated guesses. Napoleonic code, parliament, natural rights...The answers were fitting together.

The true and false section turned into a guessing game. He never liked true and false questions, even when his brain was at its best. It always seemed like there was a trick word planted to deceive him.

By the time Brayden got to the definition section, his mind started to wander. What was Waterloo? Willow would have laughed at that word and thought he made it up. She probably would have written it into one of her stories. The words on the page began to blur. He tried to refocus, but couldn't seem to get a good grasp on his thoughts. Maybe he should rest for a few minutes. He positioned himself so it looked like he was still working, shielded his eyes and relaxed. He didn't stir until a chair scraped against the floor when Maya got up to turn in her test.

Brayden answered a few more questions, but by that time, most of the students were walking up to the front. He looked at the clock and discovered that the two-hour time limit was almost over. At least he could finish the test later. The bell rang and the students exploded out of their seats, flocking to the door.

"Did you have a good nap?" Victoria asked in a sticky sweet voice. "Hate to see *your* grade."

"Good thing that's my business," Brayden retorted.

Trey overheard. "You fell asleep? Oh, man. That stinks. Maybe they'll go easy on you, considering all that's happened."

"Yeah, maybe."

"I know we have an extra-long lunch break, but I'm starving. Do you want to go eat now?" Trey asked.

"Sure."

Trey bought three pieces of pepperoni pizza and a Coke from the ala carte line and they sat at their table. Ian and Parker showed up right after them with crinkled paper lunch sacks. Ian's right ankle was wrapped in a white ace bandage. He was limping dramatically.

"What's up with your leg?" asked Max.

"I twisted it last night when I was running on the trail."

"Is it sprained?" Brayden asked.

"Nah. It actually felt fine this morning, but I figured I'd try milking it for some sympathy."

Trey smacked his arm. "That's lame."

"Hey, it seems to be working for Brayden," Ian protested. "He even has Kenzie talking to him. And my guess is the teachers will take it easy on him during finals. That would sure help me out this week."

"That's 'cuz he's actually hurt and had a sister die in a tornado. Not quite the same category as a sore ankle that's not even sore anymore," Trey said.

Parker pounded Ian on the back. "If it works for you, let me know. I might come with crutches tomorrow or something."

Brayden's head started to ache. It almost always seemed to ache when he hung around with Parker and Ian. He dug into his paper lunch sack, and pulled out a meat sandwich, chips, and five Oreos.

"I guess you don't have to worry about cutesy notes in your lunch anymore," Ian stated.

Trey tried to punch his arm, but Ian blocked him.

"Do you ever think before you talk?" Trey asked. "It's like you have no filter."

"What? I was just making an observation."

Max and Gavin joined them.

"Observation about what?" asked Gavin.

"Never mind," said Trey. "It's not worth repeating."

"Big surprise there," said Max. He dropped his soft pretzel and cheese dipping sauce on the table. "I think I've already fried my brain and we only have one final down."

Brayden rubbed the sides of his head. The pressure was building.

"Are the finals already getting to you, too?" asked Max.

"Ian's what's probably getting to him," said Trey.

Brayden stuck his hands under the table. "I'll be good in a minute."

"What's your definition of good?" asked Ian. "You've been like a walking zombie ever since the tornado."

Trey sprang to his feet and bent down, almost touching Ian's beaked nose with his own. "You've been on my nerves all day. I need you to stop talking."

Ian stood up mere inches away from Trey. "I can talk all I want."

Trey shoved him. "No. You can't. Not around me."

Ian shoved him back, even harder. Trey swung out his arm to catch himself and accidentally hit Brayden in the face.

Trey spun around. "Sorry, Brayden. Are you okay?"

Brayden's head was ringing, but he nodded.

"No, you're not," said Max. "Your head is bleeding."

Brayden touched his stitches and looked at his hand. His fingertips were covered in blood.

"Oh, no!" Trey exclaimed. "I'll take you to the nurse. I need to get away anyhow--before I punch someone on purpose."

Brayden covered his scar with his hands as they walked to the office. Crowds parted quickly when they saw the blood. Trey steered him onto the bed in front of the nurse.

"Did I pop his stitches?" Trey asked.

The nurse slid her rolling chair over to Brayden and looked at his forehead. She turned to Trey. "You hit him on his cut?"

160

"Not on purpose," said Brayden. "He was falling and just reached out to catch himself. I was in the way."

"Hmm," the nurse said. She pulled see-through latex gloves out of a box by the sink and snapped them onto her hands. "That is one serious cut." She tore an alcohol pad from its wrapper and dabbed at his stitches. Brayden cringed and pulled back. She paused for a moment until he held still again.

"Did I break him open again?" Trey asked.

"No. He's still in one piece." The nurse looked closer. "We're in luck. All of the stitches are still holding. I'm going to call your mom, just so she keeps an eye on you this afternoon."

"Eww. That would be disgusting," Trey said.

The nurse didn't smile.

"Sorry." Trey looked at his feet. "Just trying to lighten the mood."

Brayden grinned. "Thanks."

The nurse covered his stitches with gauze and medical tape. "The next set of finals start in seven minutes. Do you think you can take the next one, or do you need to stay here?"

Brayden's head was still aching, but he didn't want to miss the final. "I think I'll head to class."

"Any problems and you come right back," she commanded.

"Got it."

"I'll walk you to your next test. I owe it to you after smacking you in the head," Trey said. "What final do you have?"

"Algebra II."

They gathered books from their lockers and Trey cleared a path by extending his dark, muscled arms to either side. "Coming through," he announced. "Make way."

The crowd parted, turning to stare at Brayden. He fingered his new bandage self-consciously. The nurse was very generous with the gauze and tape.

"Good luck," Trey said when they reached the classroom door.

"Same to you." Brayden turned in his math book and eased into his desk.

"What happened to you?" asked Kenzie.

Brayden tried to smile. "Well, I was in this tornado and—"

"Very funny. I mean with your stitches wrapped again. You didn't have bandages this morning."

"You noticed?" Brayden was oddly pleased.

"Sure, I noticed. Hard to miss when it's right in the middle of your forehead."

"Oh. Yeah." Brayden's pleasure waned.

"Sooo...Are you going to tell me what happened?" Kenzie asked.

"Trey punched me in the head."

"What? I thought you were friends. Of course, I always thought you hung around with a bunch of self-absorbed bullies, but—"

"He didn't mean to hit me," Brayden clarified. "He was falling backwards and accidentally hit me when he was trying to catch himself."

"Oh. I see." Kenzie blushed. "So are you okay?"

"My head's ringing, but that's not terribly new."

"Are you going to be able to take your test?"

"I'm going to try." Brayden smiled. "I can't let the study guide you gave me go to waste."

Kenzie smiled back. "Good to hear."

The bell rang and Mrs. Brinkhaus shut the door. "Clear you desks except for your pencil and a piece of scratch paper so you can work out your problems."

Brayden's eyebrows went up. He tore a blank sheet out of his black journal and placed it on his desk.

Mrs. Brinkhaus handed out the tests. "You may begin."

Brayden tried to ignore the pounding in his head. The medical tape pinched his skin causing another distraction. He sighed and read the first math problem. $(8-2i)(5+i)=$. Even with a headache he could solve that one. He breezed through two more problems, but questions gradually increased in difficulty. He was glad he had reviewed the study guide. More head pounding. He gritted his teeth, determined not to give up.

Three more problems done. The medical tape was itchy. He was glad the stitches didn't rip out. Trey would have really felt bad then. He appreciated Trey standing up for him with Ian, but he felt like a wimp not doing it himself. What was Ian's problem? He recalled their conversation. Did Ian actually think he was using his injury to get attention? Only Ian would be a big enough loser to try to copy an injury. The comment about the note in his lunch from Willow was annoying, too. He pictured the tiger note she gave him and his head started to spin. No, she wouldn't be able to send him more notes, and Ian was a jerk to bring it up. He rubbed his head. And then Ian said that he had been a zombie ever since the tornado. Was that true? Even if it was, Ian had no right to insult him. Not with Willow dying and his head being nearly cut in two.

Brayden stared at the math page. He tried to stuff his frustrations in so he could concentrate and work on his final, but the pain was too much. The journal page. The counselor had suggested writing his thoughts down so his head would stop pounding.

He clenched his pencil even tighter and stared at the blank piece of paper. What should he write? He tried to focus on releasing his torment through his writing. The counselor said to let it out instead of stuffing it in like he usually did. The pencil started to quiver in his hand. He dropped it in alarm and looked around. No one noticed.

He picked up the pencil again, and tried to write a sentence about how he felt. This time the pencil began to spin in his hand. The journal page blew off his desk. He felt an instant relief in his head. Shocked, he threw down the pencil again. The kid sitting beside him looked up briefly, but returned to work.

How bizarre. He grabbed the journal page. Maybe he would experiment with releasing his emotions more later when he didn't have an audience. He tried to return his focus to math, but was too stunned to get very far. The bell rang.

Kenzie followed him out of the classroom. "How did you do?"

"I started off well."

"And then your head started hurting, didn't it. I saw you, you know."

Brayden stopped. "You did?"

"Yeah. You don't have to hide it. It's very understandable."

"It is?"

"Sure. You're pain is nothing to be embarrassed about. I saw you rubbing your head. You don't have to try and hide it."

"Oh. Right." Brayden started walking again. But was there something else he *did* need to hide?

CHAPTER 19

BRAIN STORM

Brayden stopped by the counselor's office after school. She was sitting in her spinning chair, looking over the manila file folder containing his tests.

"Have a seat," she instructed.

Brayden dropped into the purple chair.

"How do you feel you're doing on finals so far?" Mrs. Patel asked.

"I seemed to remember some of what I studied, so that was good. About midway through the first test I guess I fell asleep. And then during the second test, I had a hard time concentrating and my head started spinning again."

"Did you try journaling?"

"Yes."

"And did that help? Were you able to release your frustrations enough to get back to the test?" Mrs. Patel scooted forward in her chair.

"Um. I guess I released *something*, but I didn't get much more done on my test."

"Maybe you could practice writing in your journal at home first, so you get used to it," she suggested.

"I think I will."

Mrs. Patel beamed. "Good. I appreciate your positive attitude." She handed him the file. "Just return the completed tests to me in the morning."

"Got it. Thanks."

Brayden biked home quickly, eager to be alone. He swung off his bike. It crashed to the garage floor, but he was in too much of a hurry to pick it up. He burst through the door.

"How was school?" asked his mom. "Were you able to do your finals?"

"Sort of." Brayden grabbed an apple and ran up to his room.

"Is everything all right?" she called after him. "And why is your head bandaged again? I thought you unwrapped it this morning."

"I'm fine. I just need more time with a bandage. I'll be down soon. I need to finish my tests," he hollered before shutting the door.

He dropped his backpack on the bed and yanked open the zipper. Questions raced through his mind. What made his pencil spin? Could he have controlled it with his mind? Did he mentally make the paper blow off the table? He pulled out the manila folder and his black journal. His desk was covered in a jumble of old school papers, sympathy cards, Reese's Peanut Butter cup wrappers (his favorite) and a dirty black sock. He dug through the stack until he uncovered a pencil and then brushed everything else onto the floor, replacing them with the tests and journal.

He took a deep breath and concentrated on the pencil in his hand. Nothing moved. Maybe he needed to actually write something. He sat up straight and wrote his name in big block letters across the top of the page. The pencil did not budge. Disappointed, he hunched down and wrote about wishing school was over. Still nothing. Had he only imagined the pencil moving at school?

Brayden shoved the journal aside and pulled out his tests. He returned to his backpack and grabbed his study guides. His excitement dissipated when he stared at the finals. Why was he disappointed when he should be relieved? The spinning pencil was probably something his stress-induced mind imagined. It should be reassuring knowing nothing unusual was actually happening to him.

A couple hours later, Mom knocked on his door. "Hey, Brayden? Are you ready for dinner?"

He looked at the clock, surprised that he had managed to work for so long without zoning out again. His World History final was done, and he only had two more math problems to finish.

"I'll be right down."

He worked for a few more minutes and walked downstairs.

"What's for dinner?"

"Chicken casserole," Mom answered.

"Again?"

"We still have a freezer full of food from family and friends. It may take a while for us to get through it all." Mom's eyes twinkled. "But don't worry. We'll get back to eating healthy, unusual food soon."

"Great. Something to look forward to," Dad said.

Mom prayed and they dug into their casserole and salad.

"At least this is good," Brayden commented, licking his fork.

"Most of it has been great," said Dad. "And we've had lots of meat, and I recognized almost everything I ate." He turned quickly to his wife and stammered. "None of it was as good as your cooking, of course."

Mom narrowed her eyes and gave him a warning turn of her head.

"So, how are the tests coming along?" asked Dad, eager to change the subject.

Brayden gave an exaggerated sigh. "I'm tired of working on them, so I'm quitting for the night."

"You're quitting?" Mom asked. "Can't you give it one more try? It would sure help your grades if you could complete your finals. Do you need help?"

"I don't think you're supposed to help me." Brayden grinned. "I don't need help anyhow. I just finished."

"Finished? You finished both of your finals? Do you feel good about how you did?" asked Dad.

"Good enough. I'm just relieved that I can finish something. I was beginning to wonder if my brain was too scrambled to do much of anything."

Mom jumped up from the table and pulled a towel off a circular object. "We can celebrate your unscrambled brains with some thawed cherry pie. I didn't make it so I'm sure Dad will love it."

This particular pie was burnt around the edges and had an interesting color and aroma.

"Who made this one?" asked Dad.

"Your Aunt Marge."

"I think I'm actually stuffed," Brayden said.

"Me, too," Dad added.

"Oh, no you don't. She's going to ask how it was, and we need to be able to give her an answer." Mom cut the pie into generous wedges and placed a slice on each plate.

"Can we at least have a scoop of ice cream on top?" Brayden asked.

"I guess." Mom dug through the freezer and topped each slice of pie with a scoop of vanilla ice cream.

Dad took a bite and gagged, eventually spitting the bite of pie into his napkin. Brayden watched his reaction and avoided the pie, going straight for the ice cream.

"No, sir. We all have to try it. You know Aunt Marge. She *will* ask about it," Mom said.

"We also know Aunt Marge's cooking," Brayden said. "Can't you just tell her I'm on a limited diet from my injury?"

"We'll try it together," Mom said.

Brayden rolled his eyes. "Fine."

They each scooped a bite of pie on their forks, watching each other carefully.

"Ready?" asked Mom.

Brayden nodded.

Dad was smiling. "I'll count for you. One, two, three. Eat it."

Brayden and Mom both stuck the pie in their mouths. Brayden grimaced and swallowed quickly. He took a huge bite of ice cream to remove the after-taste. Mom closed her eyes while she chewed.

"Are you savoring it?" asked Dad.

She ignored him, swallowed and drank her entire glass of water.

"So what should we tell Aunt Marge?" Dad asked.

A loud clatter interrupted Mom's answer. They spun around. Banjo had pulled the pie onto the floor and was devouring it.

"Stop, Banjo," Mom said without moving.

"Yeah, stop," said Dad, still smiling.

Banjo licked the tin pie plate clean.

"Bad dog," said Brayden, petting Banjo's head.

"I guess we tell Aunt Marge that Banjo loved the pie." Mom said. "Anyone want more ice cream?"

Two more days of finals lumbered by without incident. Brayden was both relieved and disappointed that no pencils spun and no paper blew off his desk. If he could endure two more finals, he would be free for the summer.

He swung by the office to drop off the previous day's tests. Mrs. Patel wasn't in her room yet, so he placed them on her desk. She entered just as he was leaving.

"Oh, Brayden. Sorry I'm running late. Another successful night finishing finals?"

"Yeah. But I was wondering what I should do about the finals I have today. I mean, with it being the last day of school and all."

"If you need time to finish them tonight that isn't a problem. You can still turn them in tomorrow. School may be out, but it's a work day for teachers and staff. I'll be here, and will make sure the tests still get to your teachers."

"Good. Thanks," Brayden said.

"Not a problem. Keep up the good work. You've almost made it."

Brayden nodded and walked out the door. He collided with Ian, sending both of their books sliding across the floor.

"Way to go, klutz," Ian snarled. He looked up. "Oh. Brayden."

"Ian."

They both bent down and gathered their books.

"So is this your new hang out?" asked Ian. "I saw you coming out of here a couple times yesterday, too."

"I'm just checking in."

"Are you going all mental on us or something?" Ian asked.

Brayden's jaw tightened. "What are you doing here? Getting your head examined?"

"Nah. *My* brain's fine. Coach is making me get a note from the nurse so I can sit out on the P.E. final."

"Why do you want to skip it? Everyone knows there's nothing to that final. You basically show up, do what he tells you and you pass."

Ian leaned forward. "But if I do it, my time getting sympathy for my leg is over," he said in a hushed voice. "Besides, I might as well kick back and relax while I can."

"If the nurse unwraps your ankle, she's going to know nothing is wrong with it."

"Quiet!" Ian said, looking around. "Don't blow it for me." He pointed to his leg and continued. "I 'lost' the clips and tied the wrap in a super tight knot. She's not going to want to bother getting it off. I'll have my note in no time."

Brayden shook his head. "Is it really worth limping around just to get special treatment?"

"You tell me. Is holding your head and moaning still helping you?"

"I'm not faking it." He felt like holding his head and moaning right now.

Ian was still talking. "Maybe not, but you've got the whole school feeling sorry for you. I might as well join in the fun for the last day. Tomorrow I can get rid of the wrap and do whatever I want."

"Have fun with that," Brayden said as he walked out of the office.

He barely avoided a collision with the yearbook editor.

171

"Thanks for the microscopic interview," he said. "We had to fill the rest of the yearbook page with student quotes on what they liked about high school."

"Sounds interesting," Brayden commented.

"No. It really wasn't. There's only so many times you can write about going to the pool or looking for a job."

"I just wasn't ready to talk about it," Brayden explained.

"Yeah. Well, it doesn't matter now. I've already turned everything in. The tornado will be old news by next year."

Brayden's headache intensified and the hallway started to distort. He leaned against the cinder block wall to regain his balance. His life was drastically changed forever, but his classmates could move on as if nothing had happened. The tornado was becoming old news. A mild inconvenience as roads were repaired and a few homes and stores were rebuilt. His stitches would be gone one day. Maybe his scar would fade. His brain might even untangle itself. But he would always miss his sister.

CHAPTER 20

THINNING FLOOD

A slender hand patted his back. "Brayden? Are you all right?"

He shook his head, trying to clear the double image wavering in front of him.

"You're not okay?" a voice asked. "Do you want me to take you to the nurse?"

Brayden squinted until the two images became one. It was Kenzie. She really did have pretty eyes.

"Are you with me? Do you need to sit down?"

He concentrated on stuffing the spinning inside so he could focus on what she was saying. He should say something. She expected him to answer. "No. I'm fine." His knees gave out and he slid to the floor.

"This is what fine looks like?" asked Kenzie. She sat beside him on the concrete.

"You don't have to wait with me," Brayden said, though his mind was begging her to stay. "I don't want to make you late to class."

She looked at her silver bracelet watch. "We still have six minutes. We're fine."

"This is what fine looks like?" Brayden tried to grin.

"I thought you were doing better. The last two days you seemed almost..."

"Normal? Like I wasn't walking on a ship in a storm? Like my mind wasn't drifting to another planet?"

"Is that how you feel?" Kenzie asked. Concern floated across her face, settling in her eyes.

"Sometimes. I've been doing better, though."

Ian limped by. "Work it, Brayden." He waved a note from the nurse at them and continued limping towards the gym.

Kenzie snorted. "I can't believe you hang out with that guy. All the girls know he's faking being hurt. He sometimes forgets to limp when he's in a hurry."

Brayden actually chuckled. He felt much better and got to his feet. Kenzie joined him.

"Which final do you have now?" she asked.

"Spanish."

"Do you think you can get through the test?"

"Probably."

"Do you need help getting to class?"

"Probably." Ian already accused him of using his injury for sympathy, so he might as well. She did offer.

They passed by Trey, Max and Gavin, who elbowed each other, but managed to keep quiet. Max gave a thumbs up sign, but Kenzie didn't notice.

"See you in English," she said.

"Yeah. Thanks, Kenzie."

She nodded and rushed off to her class. Brayden was still smiling when his teacher delivered the finals.

"You're looking better today," she commented.

174

"Oh. Yeah."

He began scribbling down answers on his test. He still had trouble focusing, but this time it wasn't because of pain or frustration. Who could have guessed that Kenzie actually cared about him?

The bell finally rang. Brayden handed the teacher his nearly-completed test and rushed to English.

Max stopped him outside the door. "What's the hurry? Are you eager to get your last final done, or are you hoping to see a certain someone again?"

Brayden pushed him aside, but chuckled.

"It's me, right?" Trey asked, stroking his freshly-shaved head. "You couldn't wait to see me again? Don't worry. I'll be right in."

There was a line at Mr. Hankenson's desk. Students were handing in *The Hiding Place* books. Brayden scanned the crowd, finally spotting long, black hair. Kenzie smiled at him as she returned to her seat. Brayden grinned back as he inched his way up in line.

"I'm glad you stuck out the year," Mr. Hankenson said as he checked off Brayden's book.

Brayden nodded and returned to his chair. Logan was sitting sideways in his seat, nervously chewing his pencil eraser. Sweat glistened on his acne-ridden forehead.

"You're not worried about this test, are you?" asked Brayden. "You're like the smartest kid in this class."

Logan turned around. "Are you talking to *me*?"

"Yes."

"Are you insulting me?"

Brayden's eyebrows shot up. "No."

"That's new. But since you asked, I need to do well on this test."

"Don't you always do well?"

"Yes." Logan wiped his forehead with his sleeve. "But that's just it. I have straight As so far. I need to get an A in here, too."

"You have straight As this quarter or this whole year?" asked Brayden.

"I've had straight As my whole life. Or at least, since they started giving letter grades instead of Excellent, Satisfactory, and Unsatisfactory."

"Your whole life?" Brayden's eyes widened. "I had one quarter when I had all As except for one B in math or something. My dad nearly had a heart attack. So when teachers were giving E, S, or U's you probably had all Es too, huh?"

Logan shook his head and looked down at the floor. "I got one S during the last quarter of kindergarten. My mom was so mad she locked me in the closet for hours. She is a perfectionist."

Brayden's jaw dropped. "I'll say. That's harsh. Sorry, man."

Logan nodded. "I'm sorry for all you've gone through, too. No one deserves losing a family member. My mom is difficult, but I still can't imagine her dying."

The bell rang just as Max and Trey slid into their seats.

"Miss us?" Trey asked.

"You know the drill," said Mr. Hankenson. "Clear your desks and let's get started. I know you're all ready for this class, this week, and this year to be over."

Mr. Hankenson started handing out the finals on the opposite side of class.

Max tapped Brayden on his shoulder. "Duck," he whispered.

Brayden turned just as a spitball flew past his face, hitting Logan on the back of the head.

Max handed the straw to Brayden. "Our last chance for spitballs until next year."

"During a final? That's not cool," Brayden said.

"*Before* the final. We'll stop once he gets his test." Max snatched the straw back and gave it to Trey. "Never mind. Trey will do it."

Mr. Hankenson was walking closer. "Is there a problem guys? Just because you don't have your test yet, doesn't mean you can talk."

Brayden could feel Max's eyes boring into the back of his head, but chose to ignore the sensation. Mr. Hankenson dropped a final in front of him. Time to focus.

He answered several questions and then glanced up. The spitball Max shot was still stuck in Logan's hair. It would probably distract Logan if he flicked it out. Logan's mom locked him in the closet as a kindergartener--just for not having perfect grades. And here he and his friends had targeted him for years without knowing the full story. Brayden felt a surge of anger. He was annoyed at himself and his friends, and with Logan's mom. The pages of his test rippled. He looked around. Now was not the time! He concentrated on stuffing his anger inside so he could get through this last final. His test blew onto the floor.

His eyes strayed to the clock. He had to contain himself for another hour. He reached for his final and took three deep breaths. When he opened his eyes, he noticed Kenzie was watching him. He smiled at her reassuringly until she returned to her test.

Students began counting down. He looked at the clock. There were fifty-four seconds left in the school year. Relief flooded over him and he joined in the counting. The bell rang in triumph and students swarmed the desk, throwing their tests on top. The crowd pushed him into the hall. He looked for Kenzie, but the flood of people was moving too fast.

"Clear the way!" yelled a senior. He jumped on his skateboard and rolled down the center of the hallway.

Brayden laughed as he jumped to the side. Students threw papers in the air, hollered and ran through the halls. The shackles of school were released for the summer. He strolled to his locker for the last time and crammed its contents into his backpack.

The mob surged to the front doors. Brayden wanted to follow them. He was tempted not to pick up the finals, especially since he had almost finished them this time. He looked over heads, searching for Kenzie or some of his friends. The crowd was too thick to find them.

At the last minute, he made a detour into the office. Mrs. Patel handed him the manila folder with the last two tests inside.

"You did much better on the tests this time," she said. "These shouldn't take you long. See you tomorrow."

"See you."

A dramatic howl made him jump and drop the folder. His tests fluttered to the floor. Parker and Gavin stumbled to the nurse's office, half carrying, half dragging a distraught Ian. They dropped him onto the cot.

"I think my ankle is broken!" Ian cried. He rolled back and forth, clutching his wrapped foot.

"Calm down and hold still," the nurse commanded. She felt his ankle. "I can't tell what's wrong with it wrapped so tight. How did you reinjure it? Why did you have to tie your bandage into a triple knot? We'll have to cut it off just to examine you."

Brayden picked up his tests and poked his head in the door. "Are you okay, Ian?"

"Does it look like it?" Ian asked. "Some crazy senior ran into me on his skateboard. I think I broke my ankle."

Brayden tried to keep a solemn face. "Are you *sure* you're hurt?"

Ian groaned. "This time it's for real. Come look for yourself!"

The nurse stopped cutting his bandage. "This time? What do you mean? Were you faking an injury earlier?"

Ian's head rolled back. "What does it matter now? I'm dying here."

The nurse shook her head and finished cutting. The bandage fell to the floor. She gently examined his leg and ankle. Ian's howling grew louder.

"Well, it looks like you'll be limping a while longer," she said. "I'm guessing you have a sprain and possibly a break. I'll call your mom so she can take you to get x-rays." She helped him elevate his leg on a pillow and pulled an icepack out of the mini fridge in the corner. "At least you won't need any notes to get out of P.E."

Brayden bit his lip. "Do you want me to stay with you while you wait for your mom?"

"Actually, these two boys can do that. Can you get his books out of his locker?" asked the nurse. She turned to Ian. "Write down your locker combination."

"The teachers always tell us to never give away our locker combinations," Ian said, writhing in pain.

"What is it going to matter now?" asked the nurse. "You'll have a different locker next year."

"Oh. Yeah."

She thrust a pencil and paper in front of him so he could scribble down the numbers. Brayden dropped his own backpack to the floor and ran out the office door. Kenzie dodged out of the way.

"Sorry," he said. "That's the third time I've done that today."

"That wasn't you howling in there, was it?" Kenzie asked.

"No. That was Ian. He hurt his ankle. The nurse wants me to go get his stuff out of his locker."

"Ian hurt his ankle? For real this time?" She giggled and then tried to stifle it. "I'm sorry. But you have to admit, that's ironic."

"Tell me about it. Did your friends already leave?"

"Yeah. I told them to go on ahead. I just wanted to make sure it wasn't you wailing." Kenzie blushed. "So I guess I should go catch up with them."

"I guess. Thanks for checking...you know...to make sure I was okay."

"No problem. Maybe I'll run into you some this summer," Kenzie said.

"I hope so. I mean, I'm good at running into people. Especially today."

Kenzie smiled. "True. Well, bye, Brayden." She turned and walked to the front door.

Brayden waved and watched her leave. He almost wished they had another day of school so he could see her again. Almost. He ran against the thinning flood of students to get Ian's backpack.

CHAPTER 21

SPINE-CHILLING

Mom wrapped Brayden into a big hug the moment he opened their door. "You made it through the school year! I'm so proud of you."

"I still have two more final exams."

"But you're done going to school," Mom insisted.

"Tomorrow I have to go back to school to turn the finals in to the counselor."

"Okay. Okay. But technically, school is over."

"I guess," Brayden admitted.

"So, what do you want to do to celebrate?" Mom asked.

Brayden thought for a moment. "I want to eat too much pizza and chocolate chip cookies—that are made by you, not Aunt Marge or anyone else--and then I want to watch a horror movie marathon until I can't stay awake any longer."

"Oh. All right then," Mom said. "That sounds...great. I'll give Dad your pizza request and I'll start making the cookies while you finish your finals. Feel free to change your mind about the horror movies."

"Nope," said Brayden as he walked upstairs. "Sometimes a creepy movie just sounds good. And please don't try anything healthy with the cookies. No whole wheat flour or other surprises, okay?"

"No promises."

"Mom!"

"I'm kidding. For tonight only I will keep the cookies completely unhealthy for you."

"Thanks."

Dad walked through the garage door several hours later, carrying two pizzas and a bag of breadsticks. He sniffed the air and smiled. "Chocolate chip cookies?"

"That's right," said Mom. "Brayden's request."

Brayden strolled into the room, waving the manila folder. "Guess what I just finished?"

"You're finals? So soon?" Mom asked.

"I didn't have much left to do. It feels good to be done, though." Brayden sat at the table and opened one of the pizza boxes. "Three-meat pizza. Yes!" He piled three pieces on his plate.

"Save some for me," Dad said. "Mom made me get a vegetarian pizza, too. You need to help her eat that one."

Brayden shrugged and stuck a vegetarian piece on top of his pizza stack. Mom prayed and began to eat. Cheese stretched and sauce dripped as they discussed the day. When only two slices of vegetarian pizza remained, they headed to the family room to eat cookies and watch movies.

Dad scrolled through the movie options. "How about an action or adventure movie?"

Brayden shook his head. "Nope. Tonight I'm craving horror movies. Something totally disturbing. The guys have been talking about some good ones at school. If you give me the remote, I can find one."

Dad reluctantly handed over the remote control. Brayden selected a movie with a sinister doll pictured on the promotion and turned off the lights. Eerie music played right from the start.

Brayden kicked back on the recliner. "The only thing that would make this better would be popcorn."

"I'll make it," Mom and Dad both volunteered at once.

"Do you want me to pause the movie so you don't miss anything?"

"No. That's okay," Mom said.

They took their time walking up the stairs. Brayden was well into the movie before they returned.

"Air popped popcorn? Why didn't you just use the microwave kind? It would have been quicker."

"We didn't mind," said Dad. "There wasn't a rush."

Mom and Dad huddled together on the couch, munching on their own bowl of popcorn. The movie grew quiet as a teenager walked through the house with a flashlight, grumbling about the power being out. A quiet, scraping sound...and then a tiny hand grabbed the teen's ankle.

A shrill, piercing scream split the darkened room. It didn't come from the T.V. Dad cleared his throat and tried to collect himself. "It's okay, honey," he said, patting Mom's leg. He began to pick up the popcorn that now littered the room.

"Don't pass that scream off on me," she retorted. "We all know that was you."

Brayden laughed. "Wow, Dad. I didn't know you scared so eas...Aaah!"

Spine-chilling music intensified as the little doll attacked the teen's best friend. Brayden tried to look away, but was transfixed. He didn't even notice when his parents crept out of the room and escaped upstairs.

When the movie finally ended, Brayden decided one scary show was enough for the night. He headed to his room, tensing every time the stairs creaked. The lights were all off. He quickly flipped them back on. They would just have to stay on until morning, even if it meant Mom complaining about energy bills. The door to Willow's room was wide open. Brayden shielded his eyes and sped down the hall. Seeing one of her old dolls now would not be helpful. He crawled into bed without even changing out of his clothes. A quick check showed that every part of his body was tucked under his blanket so cold fingers would not have access to his arms or legs.

Footsteps.

He was certain he heard faltering footsteps creeping around in the hallway. The steps were accompanied by occasional clicking noises. The suspicious sounds were getting closer. His door inched open slowly. He sucked in his breath. A hand inched its way in, feeling his bedroom wall, slithering closer to his bed.

"Aaayyyh!" Brayden yelled.

A head popped through the doorway.

"Aaayyyh!" Brayden yelled even louder.

"Okay. I know I already washed off my makeup, but I don't look *that* scary," Mom said.

"What are you doing? Why the creepy hand thing? Did you and Dad think it'd be funny to scare me?"

"I thought you were asleep. You left all the lights on, so I was just going around turning them off. You even left your bedroom light on, so I was feeling around for the light switch."

"The lights were left on for a purpose," Brayden protested.

"Why?" A smile spread across her face. "Because of your scary movie? I am so glad we left."

"Yeah. Well, leave my light on please."

She came in and switched on his desk lamp. "That should be good enough. If you leave the main light on, you won't sleep."

"I might not sleep anyhow."

Mom attempted an evil laugh. "Good night. I hope you survive until morning." She walked out and closed the door.

"Not funny."

His eyes adjusted to the dim light. A pile of clothes in the corner of his room bore an uncanny resemblance to a doll hiding under a blanket. He knew all of Willow's dolls were in her room, but his mind fixated on the pile anyhow. There would be no sleep until the pile was gone. He finally worked up the courage to throw the clothes in his hamper. When he stood up, he found that he was dizzy and he quickly sat back down. His head ached. He squeezed his eyes shut; only opening them long enough to make sure nothing had moved. At last, he drifted into a troubled sleep.

He dreamed that he was in Willow's room, looking for one of her dolls. Willow was crying because she couldn't find it. He grabbed a flashlight and they both flopped onto their stomachs so they could look under her bed. Willow saw her doll and was excited. She started to reach for it, but jerked her hand back when it smiled at her. They both ran out of the room. Brayden looked back. The doll was chasing them. He looked back again. This time, there was a tornado chasing them. It was getting closer and closer. They both screamed as it swallowed them and sent them spinning in the air. Willow was screaming his name, asking him to save her.

He tried grabbing her ankles, but his fingers were slipping. He kept spinning until he felt sick.

Suddenly, he was back in his own room.

Willow and the creepy doll were gone. He exhaled, relieved to find it was all a nightmare. His head ached, but when he rubbed it to relieve the pressure, he was startled to find his hair blowing. Was the ceiling fan on? He tried to turn it off, only to find he could not touch the ground. He was spinning in the air. His blanket and sheet whirled around him, whipping his arms and legs. Was he still dreaming after all? He reached for a bed post and finally caught it. His legs stretched out behind him as a huge gust of wind tossed him about.

Brayden closed his eyes and took a deep breath. "Relax. Just relax," he murmured.

Gradually, the wind calmed down. His body flopped onto his bed and he opened his eyes. Was he fully awake this time? He turned his light back on. The ceiling fan was not spinning. The blanket and sheet were in a twisted heap at his feet. His headache and dizziness were suddenly gone. What was going on? Was he going crazy and imagining things, or was he turning into some kind of freak who made things spin?

The digital clock on his dresser showed 4:26 in glowing red numbers. It was pointless trying to go back to sleep now. A distraction was necessary. He dug through a pile on his desk until he found his video games. A zombie popped onto the screen. His heart jumped in his chest and he immediately turned it back off. A book would have to do for tonight.

Time seemed to stall intermittently. At 7:30, he finally took a shower and got dressed.

Mom and Dad were at the breakfast table, munching on cold cereal bathed in milk. They both looked at the clock in surprise when they saw Brayden.

"I figured you would sleep in this morning," Mom said.

"Me too, but I couldn't sleep. I figured I might as well go ahead and turn in my tests."

"Did the thought of evil dolls keep you awake?" asked Dad with a smirk.

"I found myself looking over my shoulder, making sure nothing was following me—and I didn't even watch the whole movie," Mom admitted.

Dad laughed. "It wasn't *that* scary."

"Oh, really? Then why did you let Banjo sleep with us last night?" asked Mom.

"He looked lonely."

"Sure he did. And why did you leave the bathroom light on?" Mom crossed her arms.

"Oops. I must be getting careless in my old age," Dad said.

Brayden grinned. "Good one, Dad."

"He wasn't the only one who left lights on all night," Mom said, turning to Brayden. "Seems like I remember someone screaming when I tried to turn them off last night."

"I didn't scream."

"Oh, sorry. Does that sound too girlie? You yelled then."

"Whatever."

He grabbed a handful of Honey Nut Cheerios and jammed them into his mouth, chewing loudly. "I think I'll head off now."

"Is that all you want to eat?" asked Mom.

"For now."

He crammed the manila folder into his back pack and pedaled to school. The sidewalks were bare without all of his classmates. He was too tired to care.

Mrs. Patel smiled when he entered her door. "You're here bright and early."

"Yeah. I didn't sleep well last night, so figured I might as well turn in my tests first thing in the morning." He handed her the manila folder.

She glanced at the tests. "I'll deliver these to your teachers. We're all impressed that you finished strong." She studied his face. "Why did you have trouble sleeping?"

Brayden silently debated about whether he should describe his spinning episode. "I watched a scary movie," he said at last.

"Ahh. That could do it. The last scary movie I watched was *Nightmare on Elm Street*. I was about your age and yet I still remember it. I couldn't sleep for a long time after that."

"The guys and I used to watch scary movies together. This is the first time I remember having a nightmare about it."

"Is that so? Why do you think that is?"

"Not sure." Brayden scratched his arm and looked at the poster with the Willow look-alike. "My sister was in the nightmare."

"Would you like to tell me about it?"

Brayden thought for a moment. "I don't think I'm ready. It seemed too real."

Mrs. Patel nodded.

He wanted to tell her about the spinning. He also wanted to ask why his pencil sometimes spun around. Would she think he was crazy? The clock ticked while he struggled with how much to say.

"Is there anything else you would like to talk about? I have plenty of time."

He wanted to tell her everything. A professional opinion would be very reassuring. Unless her opinion was that he was cracking up. What would happen then? Would she send him to a psychiatrist? Or worse? Would he have to be tested? She smiled reassuringly at him. It would be a relief telling her his concerns.

Instead, he heard himself say, "I think I'm good. Thanks. I need to get back home."

"If you change your mind, give me a call at the school. I'll be here all week. I'm sure your parents are also ready to listen. Whatever you're more comfortable with. Just remember not to bottle things up. It's okay to let it out."

Brayden nodded, but wondered if that was true. Letting things out seemed to be part of his problem. "Thanks, Mrs. Patel. See you next year."

"I'll look forward to it."

Brayden looked at the front of his high school. Now he was officially done with school for the year. He was free. But free to do what? There were no more distractions. Nothing to take his mind off the tornado and losing his sister. He would have all summer to dwell on the shambles the tornado had made of his life…his family…his mind.

CHAPTER 22

RAINING DOGS

It was a week into summer vacation, and Brayden was going crazy. Not crazy in the clinical sense. His brain was functioning normally. No more spinning incidents. But he was bored. No school. No little sister to torment. He had too much time to just think, which led to dwelling on his loss.

"I think I need to get a job," he told his mom.

"I don't know if that's a good idea," she said. "Maybe next summer you can work again. You need time to heal."

"The doctor finally removed my stitches. He told me that my head looked good."

"Maybe on the outside. The x-rays of your brain are still concerning. And emotionally…we're all still healing. Let's not rush into a job."

"But I'm bored. The rest of my friends are working. I want to do something." He flopped onto the couch, putting his feet on the arm rest. He plastered a pathetic pleading look onto his face.

Mom studied him for a moment and sighed. "Maybe something for a few hours a week."

Brayden sat up. "Max texted me a few days ago. He has more lawn mowing and yard work jobs than he can handle. I could team up with him."

"I don't know…"

"Just for a few hours a week," he pleaded.

"I can't believe you're actually begging me to do yard work. We have plenty of that to do around our house."

"But I don't get paid for it—at least, not beyond an allowance. I need to be able to talk about my job with the guys. There has to be something normal about this summer."

Mom looked at him as if trying to peer into his head and see if he was truly healing. "Fine. But if your head starts hurting or you get dizzy, you have to stop."

Brayden gave her a hug. "Thanks, Mom. I'll let Max know."

A couple days later, Brayden was clipping grape vines at a client's house while Max mowed. The roar of the lawn-mower made his head ring, but the distraction was worth it. He inhaled the smell of freshly-mown grass as he untangled a lawn chair from the twisting vines. The tendrils clung to the chair legs, even after being clipped.

The mower engine stopped. Max unzipped the mower's bag and dumped the grass into a yard waste bag. He wiped sweat off his forehead. "How's it going?"

"Great," Brayden said. He snipped another grape vine.

"You might not say that after you do thirty houses, but it sure beats bussing tables or washing dishes like Trey and Parker. And did you hear what Ian gets to do this summer?"

"No. What?"

"His mom went back to work, so he has to babysit his little brother and sister. I stopped by the other day. He was hobbling around on his sprained ankle trying to keep them under control. It was hilarious."

Brayden grinned. "That would be worth seeing."

Max loaded the mower onto the back of his dad's old pickup truck. "Tomorrow I have two houses lined up, but I have to get to my brother's softball game. Do you think you could do the second house by yourself? It's just a standard mow job and it's only a few blocks from your house."

"Sure."

Brayden gathered up the pruner and clippers and stuck them beside the mower. They climbed into the cab of Max's truck.

"So, are your parents letting you drive yet?" asked Max.

"No. But if the swelling in my brain keeps going down, I'll be able to soon."

"Good." Max pulled into Brayden's driveway and scribbled down the address of where he needed to mow the next day. "Enjoy. Oh, and beware of their dog," he said, smiling. "He's ferocious."

Brayden walked through the garage door. "I'm home," he called as he walked to the stairs.

"Freeze!" Mom commanded.

"What?"

"You're covered in grass clippings and your shoes are muddy. You're leaving a trail behind you. Go to the backyard and at least brush yourself off. And take off your shoes before you come back in."

Brayden did as instructed and walked back inside. "Better?"

"Yes. So how was work?" Mom asked. "That sounds like a strange question for me to ask you. It still doesn't seem like you're old enough to be working."

"It was good. I'm sore though and need a shower."

"That's for sure. Are you done for the week?"

"No. I have a mowing job tomorrow."

Mom shook her head. "Don't push too hard. Let's have that be it for the week."

Brayden stretched and popped his back. "I'm actually okay with that." He continued upstairs.

After a long shower, he returned to the kitchen. Mom was serving up hamburgers with sweet potato fries. Dad walked in the door and joined them at the table.

"Are we done with frozen meals from family and friends?" Brayden asked.

"Yes," Mom answered.

"And you let us start our own food with hamburgers? Thanks, hon," Dad said. He took a big bite into his burger. His chewing gradually slowed down. "Is there something we should know about these burgers?"

Brayden took a small bite and grimaced.

"What do you mean?" Mom asked innocently.

"They taste…unusual," Dad said.

"That's probably because they're made out of lentils," Mom said. "They're very good for you. You can even have two of these without feeling guilty."

"One is plenty," Brayden said. "At least the fries are good."

"But it's okay if you ever want to make plain old white fries," Dad said.

"Fries made out of potatoes?" Mom clarified.

"Yeah, those. Whatever you can get at McDonalds," said Dad.

"I won't fry them like McDonalds, but I guess we can have potato fries once in a while. Sweet potato fries are just healthier."

"I can tell."

Brayden turned to his dad. "I spent the afternoon working with Max."

"And how did that go?" Dad asked.

"Good. I'm sore and I have a few blisters, but I think it'll work out. I mow again tomorrow."

"Just so you keep helping out with the yard work here. Our grass needs to be mowed too."

"I will."

The family worked together to clear the partially-eaten lentil burgers and wash the dishes. They played three rounds of Dutch Blitz before heading to bed. Brayden was grateful he worked hard, because he fell to sleep easily and actually slept through the night.

The next day, Brayden pushed his lawn mower down the sidewalk for three blocks, until he reached 3140 Poplar Street. He left the mower at the end of the driveway and rang the doorbell. A little lady with graying black hair pulled into a bun answered the door.

"Hello, Mrs. Campos? I'm Brayden. I work with Max. I'm here to mow your lawn."

"Oh, yes. Go ahead and start in the front."

Braydon finally got the mower started and began to push it in a diagonal across the front yard. He was careful to avoid the purple pansy flowers that surrounded the thick trunk of an oak tree. He was feeling good about the morning until he walked through the gate to the backyard.

A four-legged terror bounded up to him, barking and baring its teeth. The beast growled and planted himself in front of the mower. All five pounds of him.

Brayden laughed. "You're the ferocious dog Max warned me about, huh?"

He bent down to pet the tiny Chihuahua's head. The dog snapped at him and stood his ground. Brayden stood back up. "Sweet little guy, aren't you?"

The back door opened. "Oh. I see you've met my Pico. Come to mommy, Pico."

The dog ran to her feet, wagging his tail. Mrs. Campos picked him up and snuggled him up to her face. "Now you be good and stay out of the way." She kissed him repeatedly and placed him on a crumpled blanket at the edge of the deck. Pico wagged his tail as she walked back inside.

Brayden started the lawn mower. Pico ran off the deck and began barking again. He planted himself in front of the machine and growled. Brayden steered around him. The little dog followed, yapping and snapping at his heels.

"This is going to be fun," Brayden muttered.

After about ten minutes of non-stop barking, he let the mower die. "Go to the deck, Pico."

Pico barked in response. Brayden reached down to pick him up. Pico bit his hand, but the thick work gloves protected his skin. He carried the squirming, snarling dog back up to his blanket on the deck. As soon as he started the mower again, Pico returned to his feet, more annoying than ever.

Brayden mowed until he had to empty the bag into a yard waste sack. Pico kept barking.

"Don't your vocal cords ever wear out?"

He reattached the bag and continued mowing. Pico snapped at his heels. Brayden clenched the mower's handles, trying to resist kicking the little dog away. His head began to spin, but he kept mowing, determined to finish the job. He finally completed the last strip and started dumping the grass into the sack. He was cringing from the pain in his head, wishing he could block out the dog's constant barking.

The wind began to sift through his hair. He brushed it out of his eyes. Gradually, the breeze grew in strength until the clipped grass began to whirl around the dog. Brayden dropped the sack, adding even more grass to the tornado. Pico tried snapping at it and then started barking louder. The spinning intensified until it swept up the dog and he began to spin with it, snarling and snapping. His little legs pawed at the wind. Brayden tried to reach into the tornado to grab the dog, but it sucked Pico higher and higher. Pico's barking turned into yelps. Brayden's headache dissipated and the spinning stopped. Brayden leaned forward to catch the falling Chihuahua just as the back door opened.

"I thought I heard Pico crying," Mrs. Campos said. She leaned over the side of the deck. "How sweet. Did you make a friend, Pico?" She walked over and removed the stunned dog from Brayden's arms. "You should feel honored, young man. Pico doesn't get along with just anyone. He normally won't let strangers pick him up." She looked around the back yard. "You did a great job. A little raking to get rid of the cut grass and you'll be done. There's a rake under the deck. I hope Max sends you every time."

Brayden forced a smile. Mrs. Campos stroked and kissed her quiet dog and went back inside. Brayden was too stunned to appreciate the peace and quiet. He pulled a rusty, blue rake out from under the deck and cleaned up cut grass tossed around by the wind. It took several minutes to scoop all of the grass back into the lawn bag. He dragged it to the driveway and pushed his mower home.

Once he completed a quick shower, he searched for his phone and texted Max.

"Sweet dog."

Max replied, "Warned you. Now u c y I didn't mind going to my bro's game."

"I quit."

"No, don't quit. We'll tackle that house together next time."

"Are there any other homes with psycho dogs?"

"No."

"Okay. C u next week."

Banjo nosed his way through the door. He jumped up on the bed and gave Brayden a thorough face washing. His breath smelled like peanut butter and his face was wet from slurping water, but Brayden didn't care.

He rubbed the beagle's bulging stomach until the dog's foot started to thump on the covers. "You may eat everything in sight, but at least you're lovable. And it doesn't take a tornado to get you quiet."

CHAPTER 23

MICROBURST

The following week, Brayden was walking to his room, when he heard muffled crying. He stopped short and looked into Willow's room. Mom was sitting on the bed, sobbing into a rainbow pillow. He stood for several minutes, unsure of whether to give her privacy or try to comfort her. Finally, he sat beside her and put his hand on hers.

She looked up with red, puffy eyes. "Oh, Brayden. I'm sorry. I try not to cry in front of you anymore. It's just…I was looking at some of the pictures on Willow's desk. She was already drawing her birthday cake." She blew her nose on a soggy tissue. "By now we would have decided on her party theme and everything. Nothing feels right. It's mid-June and I should have invitations to her friends in the mail. Willow should be bouncing off the walls getting excited about her birthday." Mom started crying again. "I can't stand the thought of her not having any more birthdays."

"I know, Mom," Brayden said. "It's all wrong."

"What do we do on her birthday?" she asked. "Do we ignore it? Do we find a distraction so it isn't so painful? Do I bake a birthday cake just to remember her?"

"I'm not sure."

"It's not fair for me to ask you." Mom said, hugging him. "I'm just not good at this. I shouldn't be the mother of a dead child. Sometimes I feel like maybe I'm getting a grip on this and then I fall apart again."

"Me, too."

Mom wiped her eyes. "I should be strong for you. What can I do to help?"

"I don't know, Mom."

"Do you want to have the guys over some time? Is there something you've wanted to do, or somewhere you've wanted to go?"

"Maybe eventually."

"Is there something I could do for you right now? Come on. It would make me feel better. I need a good distraction," Mom insisted.

"Um…you could make something to eat. Food is always good. But it can't be health food. Think dessert. With real sugar and everything."

"Sugary dessert. I'll get started right now." She hugged Brayden again and walked downstairs.

Brayden looked around. He almost never came into Willow's room any more. It was like pressing on a bruise that wouldn't heal. He studied the picture Willow drew of her birthday cake. There were three cakes, but one had a chunky star beside it. The winning selection was a rectangular cake with a mouse surrounded by flowers and flying a kite. He looked through several other pictures, but set them aside when he saw Willow's purple notebook with "Private Collection" written across the middle.

Stories from this notebook had always been off limits. He used to be curious about what was inside, but knew if he invaded her privacy she would retaliate. Now it felt like a connection to her, and he was compelled to open the cover. The first page said, "For Willow's eyes only. Do not read until I am a famous author and illustrator." A drawing of a penguin holding a book and pencil sat underneath it.

He skipped to the end of the notebook so he could see her latest writing first. The last story had a picture of a yellow bulldozer on the top. He thought for a moment and remembered the day she drew that picture. He had yelled at her for embarrassing him with the note in his lunch. Not one of his finer moments. He dropped into her wooden chair, pulled it up to the desk and began to read.

Once there was a hot pink bug car named Simone. Her last name was Volkswagen. She was a fast little car that loved zipping around the neighborhood. The other cars watched her from their driveways and honked when she passed by.

"Hello, Simone," the cars said.

They all knew she was very nice and loved to see her.

One morning, Simone's group of cars was all parked at the gas station, enjoying a nice breakfast of oil and gasoline. Buzz the Bulldozer and Hank the Tank got into a fight. The gas fumes were horrible. If someone had thrown a match between them, they would have exploded.

Simone could tell Buzz was sad when he was getting ready for driving school. She decided to cheer him up by drawing a happy picture and sticking it on his dashboard.

When Buzz got to school, his fellow bulldozer friends saw the message and made fun of him.

"Ha, ha. You have a bug car sister who loves you," one bulldozer teased.

Buzz was so mad, he blew a gasket. He drove home as fast as a bulldozer can go (which isn't nearly as fast as a bug car). He saw Simone in the driveway and honked his horn loudly at her over and over. Before she could find out what was wrong, he drove right over her with his huge bulldozer body. He flattened her. It really hurt that poor, sweet bug car.

Velma the Van felt sorry for Simone and towed her to the repair shop. The mechanics worked on her all night, but they couldn't fix her. Finally Buzz realized how much damage he had done. He gave her a drink of super oil which made her pop back to her original bug car shape. Her pretty hot pink paint was scratched, but at least she wasn't flat anymore.

He learned his lesson and decided to never be mean to the wonderful bug car again, even if he still hung around with mean bulldozers.

Brayden felt like a knife twisted in his heart. He really had been cruel to her that day. Her bulldozer description was accurate. How many other times had he been a horrible brother? Guilt overwhelmed him and stirred up a familiar dizziness. The pictures on her wall began to flutter from a gust of wind.

"Not again," he moaned.

The papers on the desk began to spin, as did the purple notebook. Brayden tried to grab them, but there were too many, and the wind was intensifying. Stuffed animals joined the spiral, their fuzzy arms and legs waving. The pictures on the wall flapped harder until the tape couldn't hold them any longer and they began spinning too.

Brayden didn't want to disturb her room. He tried backing out the door, but he stumbled when the ground seemed to lurch to the side.

Mom stepped into the room. She dropped a plate of peanut butter cookies and a glass of milk. Instead of landing on the carpet, they were sucked into the twirling collection of papers and stuffed animals.

"We've got to get out of here!" yelled Mom. "There's a microburst in our house! Down to the basement!"

Brayden grabbed his head. "I can't help it."

"Let's go!" Mom pulled his arm.

"I'm too dizzy. I can't see straight."

"I'll help you. Come on." Mom wrapped her arms around him.

"You don't understand. It's me! I don't mean to…it just happens."

"You're not making sense. We have to leave."

Brayden dropped to his knees. The image of the bulldozer was imprinted on his brain. One of his sister's pictures tore in half. Pens, pencils and markers danced in the mini-tornado. A marker smacked into his face, leaving a red welt. A hot pink shag pillow chased the pens and caught up to the crumbling peanut butter cookies. The growing havoc increased Brayden's guilt. He struggled with the relief he felt by letting the storm out, and the need to contain it to preserve Willow's room.

He closed his eyes and mentally tried to force the wind to stop. It continued to rage. He focused on taking deep breaths and relaxing. The spinning slowed down. Finally, the stuffed animals, pink pillow and purple notebook drifted to the floor. Writing utensils smacked into the walls and rolled to the carpet. The pictures and cookie crumbs fluttered like snowflakes onto the bed.

Mom leaned against the wall. "I think I've finally snapped."

"Then we both have," Brayden said.

"Were you actually…it looked like…Was that storm somehow connected to you?" asked Mom.

Brayden was still sitting on his knees. He adjusted his legs so they stuck out in front of him and leaned back against Willow's bed. "I think so."

Mom sank to the floor beside him. "What do you think happened?"

"I'm still figuring it out. I read one of Willow's stories. Have you read any of them?"

"From her purple 'Private Collection'?"

Brayden nodded.

"I've thought about it. I think I will eventually, but right now it still feels like I'm invading her privacy." She laughed. "That makes no sense. Maybe I'm just not ready. So what story did you read?"

"Her most recent one. It was about a bulldozer, which I'm sure was me."

Mom sighed. "I do remember seeing her work on that story."

"Yeah. And she was right. I did run over her like a bulldozer, and I'm sure that wasn't the first time. I felt guilty and mad at myself, and then the storm came."

"Probably just a coincidence. A very *strange* coincidence. I should make sure the rest of the house is okay. We might have lost part of the roof or something. Microbursts can be powerful."

Brayden grabbed her arm, forcing her to stay. "You don't have to check the house. I was only in this room, and it doesn't seem to go beyond the area right around me. At least it hasn't so far."

"You're making this sound like it has happened before." She rubbed her head. "This is the first time this has happened, right?"

Brayden winced. "Not exactly. Mrs. Campos's grass and a Chihuahua got sucked into a tornado while I was mowing, and my blankets and I got sucked into one after a bad dream. My pencil and paper spin sometimes if I try to journal. You can probably blame that on the counselor you called for me. She told me to let my feelings out, because holding it in makes my head hurt more. The thing is, if I don't keep it stuffed in, it seems to explode into my own personal tornado."

"Why didn't you tell me about this earlier?"

"Would you have believed me if you hadn't seen it?" he asked.

"Good point. I'm not sure I believe it even *after* seeing it." She struggled to her feet. "I need to call your Dad, and I should probably call your doctor. Maybe they can help us sort this out."

"Yeah. Maybe."

Dad came home from work early. Mom made him sit on the recliner in the living room and handed him a hot cup of black coffee. Brayden and Mom sat across from him on the sofa and explained the tornado episodes. They watched his face carefully, waiting for his reaction.

"Huh," Dad finally said.

Mom frowned. "Huh? That's it?"

"What do you want me to say?"

"More than that."

"Well, give me a minute. I'm thinking."

She crossed her arms and shook her head.

Dad turned to Brayden. "Do you remember when we searched for Willow in the cornfield? After we saw her

204

under that wool blanket…" Dad stopped for a moment as he struggled to control his emotions. "After we saw her, they carried her into the ambulance and drove away. You got so dizzy you couldn't even stand up."

"Yeah."

"And then the cornstalks started to spin. I had to help you run to the car because I thought another tornado was coming. But it only swirled around you and then stopped."

"I sort of remember," said Brayden. "But I was out of it."

"Yes, you were. And I was in shock and just figured it was part of our crazy weather. But now it sounds like it has happened at least three more times. Right?"

"Yeah," Brayden said again. "Plus a few times where stuff just blew a little."

Dad scratched his head. "And didn't those brain tests show something was off?"

"The doctors seemed concerned when they looked at the CAT scan," Mom said.

"Then I think you're right, honey. It's time to go back to the doctor."

Mom stood up shakily. "I'll call his office right now."

CHAPTER 24

STORM DAMAGE

The earliest doctor exam opening was three days later. The nurse asked Brayden to stand on the scale and then walked him and his Mom to a room decorated with circus clowns. She asked him to sit on the paper-covered exam table, stuck a thermometer in his mouth, and then proceeded to check his blood pressure.

"The doctor will be right in." She dropped his file in a folder on the door and bustled down the hall.

"Why are there so many clowns in this room?" Brayden asked. "They're creepy."

"Then I would think you would enjoy them, based on your movie preference," Mom answered. "The doctors probably treat lots of children in this room."

"I guess that's fine as long as the kids haven't watched horror movies with clowns. The doctor visit could get very traumatic. Who would actually feel reassured with clowns grinning at them while they get a bunch of shots? I'd rather go to the doctor who does my physicals each year. One of his exam rooms has cars, and I think the other one has lions."

"Tigers," Mom corrected.

"That's right. Neither of which are disturbing."

Dr. Standish rapped on the door twice, and then breezed in before they could respond. "How are we today?"

"That's what we're hoping you'll tell us," Brayden said.

"Yes, well the notes in your file are a little unclear. It mentions dizziness leading to mini-tornados." The doctor scratched his ear and raised his bushy eyebrow in confusion. "I guess I don't understand. Do you mean that you get so dizzy that you feel like you are caught in a tornado?"

"No."

"Can you explain?"

"I have episodes where I get very dizzy and my head pounds."

"That's understandable."

"And then if I bottle it up, I feel awful for a long time. If I release it, I feel better quicker but it causes a tornado."

"Causes a tornado?" Dr. Standish repeated, looking up from his notes.

"Yes."

"What do you mean by that?"

"The air spins and things that are nearby get sucked into it and start spinning too."

"Maybe in your dizzy state of mind, things just look like they're spinning," suggested the doctor.

"No. Things actually spin."

"I know it sounds crazy," Mom said, joining the conversation. "But my husband and I have actually seen it happen."

"Is that so?" The doctor looked through his notes. "You were injured in the tornado as well."

207

"Yes, but I'm doing much better now." She crossed her arms. "My husband was never in the tornado."

"I remember seeing your story on the news. You have all been traumatized by a death in your family," the doctor stated.

"True. But we're not making this up," Mom said, an edge creeping into her voice.

"I'm sure you *think* you saw a mini-tornado, but brains can play tricks on us when we're stressed and in pain."

"Over and over?" asked Brayden. "I might not have believed it the first time, but it keeps happening."

"So show me now," said the doctor, sitting down on the rolling stool.

"But it doesn't just happen when I want it to. I have to be really upset or mad."

"Aren't you upset that I don't believe you?" asked Dr. Standish.

"*I* am," Mom snapped.

"I'm getting there," Brayden admitted.

"Then release it into a tornado."

Brayden closed his eyes. He felt a twinge of dizziness. He tried to fuel his anger and then imagined writing about it. Letting it go. He opened his eyes. Nothing moved. Not even a tongue depressor or the paper on the examining table.

The doctor stifled a yawn and returned to his feet. He stuck the stethoscope into his ears and listened to Brayden's heart and then looked into Brayden's eyes with a small light. His eyebrows furrowed together like one long caterpillar as he inspected the scar on Brayden's forehead. "I just don't see anything wrong. I can order another CAT scan, but I think you might be wasting your money. I would recommend more rest—for all of you—and just allowing time to heal."

Mom pursed her lips. "Okay."

"If you notice any other problems, let me know."

Brayden nodded. The doctor scribbled into the file, clicked his pen and left the room.

"I guess we should have seen that coming," said Brayden.

"Maybe. What a waste of a co-pay." She dug through her purse in search of her car keys. "Let's go home."

Later that week, Brayden and Max teamed up to conquer mowing for Mrs. Campos. They rang the doorbell.

Mrs. Campos poked her head out. "Hello, boys." She rubbed her eyes, causing the fake lashes from one eye to slide down to her cheek. "Sorry. I fell asleep on the couch."

"We're just here to mow and trim your yard," Max said, staring at the fallen eyelashes.

"Good. And I'm glad you brought your friend. My little Pico seems to love him."

"Is that so?" Max grinned at his partner. "Brayden couldn't stop talking about Pico either. We'll go ahead and get started in the front."

Mrs. Campos slipped back inside. Brayden trimmed along the house and plants while Max mowed. Once the front was finished, they approached the back gate. Pico was already poking his tiny nose under the fence, barking and snarling.

"Is that any way to greet someone you love?" asked Max. "Scoot back. We're coming in."

He opened the gate. Pico jumped up and down, barking and nipping at the mower as Max pushed it into the back yard. Brayden followed close behind. Pico sniffed him and froze in his tracks. He yelped, stuck his tail between his legs and scampered onto the deck.

"Love, huh? Looks more like fear to me," said Max. "But whatever it is, he's out of our way, so let's get done before it wears off."

"Works for me."

Pico stuck his head through the deck rails and watched them work. Occasionally, he ventured down the steps and crept towards the trimmer. As soon as Brayden turned, the little dog raced back up to the deck.

They finished the yard quickly. Mrs. Campos walked out the back door and scooped up her dog. Her false eyelash was still stuck to her cheek. "What a good little Pico, staying quiet for your friend while he mows." She handed Brayden a check. "See you next week."

"Yes, Ma'am."

Mrs. Campos held Pico's paw and made him wave to the boys before she closed the door.

Max pushed the mower to the truck. "Any other super powers I should know about?"

Brayden's head snapped up. "What?"

"I can't believe you calmed that obnoxious Chihuahua. He's been a nightmare all summer. Do you have any other secret talents?"

"Nothing useful," Brayden said.

On the drive home, he wondered if there was any way his apparent ability to start a tornado actually *could* be useful. Maybe if he could control the outbursts, making them start and stop when he wanted. As it was, the power was just a nuisance.

Max pulled up to Brayden's house and pressed hard on the truck's old brake. "Are you going to the football meeting next week?"

Brayden shrugged. "I'm not sure."

"You *are* going to be in football again, aren't you?"

"I guess it's been a while since I thought about it."

Max accidentally released some of the pressure on the brake and the truck jolted forward several feet. "But we've been looking forward to this for years. The coach promised us more play time once we were juniors."

"Yeah. I guess."

"Hey, don't let the whole tornado thing ruin the rest of your life. Just go to the meeting."

Brayden thought for a moment. "I'll probably go, but I'm not sure about playing this year. I'll talk it over with my parents."

"I hope they talk some sense into you," Max said. "I know you'll regret it if you drop out now."

"Maybe. Are we mowing on Tuesday?"

"Yeah. See you then."

"See you." Brayden stepped out of the truck and brushed grass off his jeans before walking through the front door. "I'm home."

"Did you have fun?" asked Mom.

"I wouldn't call yard work fun, but it was okay." He pulled off his grass-stained shoes and walked upstairs. He paused when he passed Willow's room. Most of the "storm damage" was repaired. The bed was made and the stuffed animals were back in place. The crumbled cookies and milk splotches were gone. The walls, however, looked strangely bare. All of Willow's drawings and paintings that had whirled around in the gust of wind were now in a neat stack on her desk next to her purple Private Collection notebook. A knot formed in Brayden's chest. The story he read from the Private Collection was still firmly imbedded in his brain. He pictured the yellow bulldozer flattening the bug car and wished he could reverse time and treat Willow right. Why had he been such a bully to her?

He sat on the floor by Willow's door, afraid to go in the room when thoughts were whirling in his head. Was he a bully at school, too? He thought back to the power he once felt walking down the high school hallway with his friends. Did students get out of their way because of respect like he had always assumed, or was it fear? Were they powerful just because they were on the football team or was it partly because they walked on others? Did he want to be part of a team like that again?

He recalled all of the times they pushed people around or insulted them. Much of what they did was to get a laugh at someone else's expense. The spitballs. The cruel texts. Human bowling down the hall. Willow was right. He and his buddies really were bulldozers. No wonder Kenzie and her friends were so annoyed with them. They didn't seem as upset with him now. Were they just easier on him because of all he had gone through? Or was he so twisted up from the tornado that he hadn't felt like tormenting others?

The dizzy sensation crept in again. He staggered to his room, searching for his camera. Maybe he could video tape the tornado. Not only could he show it to the bushy-browed doctor for proof, he could study it himself and work on a way to control or use the power. He wanted a way to make up for the way he used to treat people. How could a tornado help?

The camera was on his pile of dirty socks. He set it to record and placed it on his desk. The wind started to lift the socks. They spun around his other dirty clothes that spiraled in the center of his room. A black shoe joined the rotation. Then a book. Then the camera.

"Oh, no!"

The camera got tangled up in a shirt as it spun. Brayden tried to grab it, but it was spinning just out of reach. He sat on the floor and closed his eyes. His chance to document this episode might be ruined, but he could still work on trying to control it. He concentrated on taking deep, slow breaths and imagined walking on a deserted beach. The cool waves rippled over his bare feet and washed his frustrations deep into the ocean. He rubbed the sore muscles in his neck. The wind tapered off into a wispy breeze playing with his hair. He opened his eyes. The camera, clothes and socks landed in a pile in front of his window.

Brayden dug through the laundry and pulled the camera out of a shirt. It was still recording. He pushed the play button and watched three seconds of spinning socks and a close-up of a green shirt.

"So, recording attempt number one is a failure. Guess I'll try again," he said.

"Are you talking to me?" asked Mom as she stopped by his door.

"No. To myself."

"Your room could use some cleaning," she said. "It looks like…"

"A tornado hit it?" Brayden finished. "It did. I just had another outburst. I tried to video tape it this time, but the camera got sucked up too."

"That was a good idea. Maybe we can catch it on tape next time and show it to that doctor." Mom pulled the clothing hamper into the middle of his room and removed the lid. "Fill it up, please."

Brayden wadded up his shirt and hurled it into the basket. "Do you think I'm a bully?"

Mom looked up quickly and studied his face. "Are you thinking about Willow's bulldozer story again?"

He nodded, and then tossed a handful of socks into the basket too.

"Is that what triggered the latest tornado?"

"I guess so."

Mom sat on his unmade bed. "There were times when you really hurt Willow's feelings. We had to ground you more often than we would have liked because of it. But you never physically hurt her."

"Would you call me a bully?"

"Most of the time I would just call you a typical brother. There might have been a few times where it went beyond that, but I wouldn't necessarily call you a bully."

"How about with other people?"

Mom thought for a moment. "I don't see you at school very often, and maybe when I'm watching you could be acting differently than normal. But I have noticed that sometimes when you get with a bunch of your friends, you seem to get…louder, and…not as careful about how your words and actions affect others."

Brayden's shoulders dropped. "Yeah. That's a nice way of putting it." He sat quietly as his mind raced ahead. Finally he asked, "Why did Willow have to die in that tornado instead of me? She was a better person. She didn't tear people down."

Mom wrapped him into a hug. "Oh, Brayden. She wasn't better, just different. You have lots of good qualities. You're smart and funny. You're a natural leader and I know that deep down you really care about people. You don't have to keep tearing people down. Make something good actually come out of the tornado. Become the person you want to be."

Brayden nodded. "The football meeting is next week. Practice starts soon."

"I just received a reminder letter about that. Do you feel like you're ready for football again?"

"I don't know. I mean, physically I might be up for it now, but I wonder if being on the football team is part of the reason I act like a bulldozer. Maybe I shouldn't go back. I don't really feel like being with the guys every day now anyhow."

"That's up to you. I think you can still be a considerate person, even if you're part of the football team, but there might be times when being with the guys makes kindness more challenging."

"I guess I have a week to decide."

"That's right." Mom looked around his room. "Do you need help cleaning up after the latest outburst?"

"No. I've got it."

He pulled one of his socks off the ceiling fan. What kind of person did he want to be? Did being on the football team work with that image?

CHAPTER 25
BREEZE DAISIES

Brayden and his parents wound up attending the kick-off meeting for football. On the drive home, Brayden silently stared out his window, oblivious to the traffic they endured or the stores they passed. Instead, he pictured the crowd cheering as he ran with a football and then dissolving into an injured look on Willow's face.

"What are you thinking back there?" Mom asked. "Did the meeting help you make a decision?"

Brayden grimaced and shook his head.

Dad looked into the rear view mirror. "I think you need the distraction. What else are you going to do this summer? You need more than mowing lawns a few days a week and playing video games."

"Maybe."

"It might help you feel like *something* in your life remained the same," Mom added. "I feel so bad that your whole world was turned upside down during that tornado."

"But what if I start acting the same as I did before we lost Willow? What if I turn into a bulldozer again?"

Mom turned in her seat so she could see his face. Compassion flooded her eyes. "If that happens, I promise to let you know and we can pull you from the team."

"What do you say?" asked Dad. "Do I still get to cheer for my son during games?"

"No pressure there."

"I'll admit it. I like you being on the football team. But it really is your choice."

Brayden stayed up late several nights debating, but he finally decided to give football a try. Every Monday through Friday, he practiced with the guys from 7:00 to 12:30. The remainder of his time was spent trying to find a way to control his microburst episodes, document them, and use them to help others.

A corner of their unfinished basement became his experiment zone. He shoved three cardboard boxes filled with old textbooks his dad refused to give away along a wall on the opposite side of the basement. Seven plastic Christmas decoration tubs, an exercise bike, and two sleds were also relocated. He brushed away cobwebs and swept the concrete floor, gaining his mom's full support of his project. Then he placed a stack of colored paper, several stray socks and his old life-sized stuffed gorilla on the floor. He used bungee cords to strap his camera to a folding chair so he could videotape his experiments.

Initially, he attempted to run to the basement whenever his head began to spin. This was a tricky process, as descending stairs when he was dizzy was a challenge. Often, by the time he made it to his testing corner, the episode was nearly over. Most of the video was unclear and ended abruptly when a sock would land on the camera. He finally managed to get a few full episodes on tape, but during a

217

longer, intense tornado the entire chair began spinning and eventually crashed into the wall, breaking the camera and losing the data.

He practiced starting gusts of wind while he was in his testing corner by thinking about the actual tornado, Willow's death, or something else that upset him. By early August he was able to initiate a small tornado half of the time. He could stop the outburst when he wanted unless he was extremely upset.

His only unanswered question was in finding a way to make his powers useful. The more he thought about it, the more he realized wind and tornados were just not very beneficial.

The one time he thought he could be heroic, ended badly. His neighbor's orange and white Persian cat was stuck in a large cottonwood tree between their houses. Pathetic meowing lured Brayden to the site. He figured a gentle shake of the tree would encourage the cat to finally climb down, or jump into Brayden's waiting arms. He closed his eyes and replayed the tornado reaching for their car, throwing them into the air, spinning them like a top.

A surge of energy coursed through his head. His chest swelled with the power. He opened his eyes and smiled when wind swirled around the tree. The branches began to sway back and forth.

"Here, Fluffy!" he called, holding out his arms. "Jump, Fluffy! I'll catch you! It's okay, girl."

The startled cat climbed higher. Really? Didn't she know he was there to save her? Brayden's frustration grew, causing the wind to increase until the branches started to thrash frantically. Leaves spun off the limbs into the air, leaving the tree stripped like a plucked chicken. The cat hissed in terror, clinging to the highest branch. Her long fur rippled and her ears pressed against her head in fear.

"Hurry, Fluffy! I've got you."

Brayden tried to calm the storm, but the wind kept blowing. The poor cat suddenly lost her grip, her little paws flailing in the air. Brayden held out his arms to catch her, but the cat began to spin and blew sideways to the far side of his neighbor's lawn.

Brayden finally stifled the storm and checked on the poor cat. One of her legs was bent in the wrong direction. He pounded on the neighbor's door and told her that the cat fell out of the tree. The very confused neighbor scooped up her cat ten feet from the bare cottonwood tree and drove her to the vet.

After that episode, Brayden decided his power was useless. He was glad he had more control over it, especially with school approaching, but determined his hope to be some kind of superhero was dead.

The last day of summer vacation, Brayden slept in until 10:30. He stretched and rolled out of bed. After throwing on shorts and a t-shirt, he meandered downstairs to the kitchen. Surprisingly, his dad was still there, sipping on coffee and reading an issue of *Harvard Business Review*. Mom pulled a second batch of homemade donuts out of the oven and flipped them onto a cooling rack.

"Would you like a donut?" she asked.

Brayden eyed them suspiciously. "How healthy are they?"

"Well, they aren't fried, so they are a little healthy," Mom answered. "But I actually put a *little* sweetener in them, so they taste good. Right, honey?"

Dad hid his face behind his magazine, pretending to be too absorbed to answer.

Mom scowled. "Okay, so the sweetener isn't sugar, it's a ripe banana, but you might like them. At least try one."

Brayden grabbed a donut and sat down. He cautiously nibbled on it, very aware that his mom was watching. The bland pastry stuck to the roof of his mouth. He swallowed hard. "It's not that bad."

Mom smiled and handed him a glass of apple juice. "Good. We have lots more." She put two on a napkin and set them by his juice. Dad chuckled behind his magazine.

Brayden waited until Mom's back was turned and then slipped one of the donuts under the table to Banjo's eager mouth. He turned to his Dad. "Why are you still home?"

Dad peered over his magazine. "I figured we could all spend the day together, since it's your last day before school starts again. What would you like to do?"

"Go scuba diving? Or mountain climbing?"

"Both of those would be hard in Kansas. How about something realistic."

Brayden thought for a moment. "Laser tag?"

"That we could do. Anything else?" asked Dad.

"Take Banjo to the dog park?"

"Good idea. Is that enough?"

There was a long pause. Dad closed his magazine and pushed it aside.

"Could we go visit Willow's grave?" Brayden suggested in a subdued voice.

"Really?" Mom stopped scrubbing the counter in surprise. "I think that is a wonderful idea."

Dad and Brayden searched for their shoes while Mom bagged up the donuts. "Anyone need another donut for the drive to laser tag?"

"I'll pass," said Dad.

"Me, too," Brayden added.

Banjo whined and strained to reach the donut bag.

"Not you," Mom said. "Though thank you for your interest. I'm glad someone appreciates healthy food."

Brayden snickered. "Banjo also likes to chew rocks in the backyard."

"Get in the car," Mom said.

Mom and Dad teamed up against Brayden at Laser Tag, but he still beat them two out of three rounds. Dad insisted that his laser gun was not working properly. Mom said her leg slowed her down too much, even though her cast and crutches were finally gone.

They returned home, ate a quick lunch and loaded Banjo into the back seat of the car. The excited beagle stuck his head out the window as they drove to the dog park. He panted, letting his tongue ripple in the wind. Strings of slobber blew through the air, adorning the windshield of the truck behind them.

Brayden removed Banjo's leash once they closed the dog park gate. Banjo howled in delight. He ran in wide circles, sniffing at a German shepherd and a dachshund, walking through mud and returning to his family pack. They strolled down to the pond. Banjo splashed in and splashed back out. He sniffed around the water's edge and started rolling on the ground.

"What are you doing?" asked Dad.

They walked closer. A dead trout was decomposing in the weeds, filling the air with a ripe stench. Banjo rolled back and forth over the fragrant fish.

"Disgusting," Mom said, plugging her nose. "Get away from that."

Dad blocked the fish while Brayden ran with the dog to the water. Banjo paddled around in the water for a few minutes. When he emerged, he shook water onto Brayden's bare legs. After walking two more times around the dog park, they all piled back into the car.

Mom spread an old towel on the seat. "Make sure he stays on that until we get home."

They all rolled down their windows as Dad drove nine miles per hour over the speed limit. They were still gasping for fresh air by the time they pulled into the driveway.

"I may never eat fish again," Dad said.

Mom stuck Banjo in the bath tub and bathed him three times. When he finally emerged, his fish aroma was at least masked by the dog shampoo.

"Do you still want to go to Willow's grave?" asked Mom as she dried her arms with a fluffy red towel.

Brayden nodded.

Mom pulled on her blue gardening gloves and went outside for a few minutes. When she returned, she held some freshly clipped pink daisies with yellow centers. "I'm ready when you are."

Brayden leaned his head against the window on the way to cemetery. Houses and buildings that had tangled with the tornado were now repaired. Even the battered trees were trying to grow new limbs to replace the gaping holes in their shape. The town was healing. He listened to his parents laughing, and smiled. They were healing too. Then he looked at Willow's empty seat and felt a familiar ache. They were healing but were not completely healed. Their lives were forever changed.

By the time they parked and walked to Willow's grave, a somber quiet fell upon them. Mom gathered the old, wilted flowers from a heavy ceramic vase and replaced them with the pink daisies. The gentle wind caressed the petals and leaves. It sent loving ripples through the tender green grass covering her coffin.

"I'm going to go throw the old flowers away and take a little walk," Mom said. She patted Brayden's shoulder. "Would you like to come along or would you like some time alone?"

"Time alone," Brayden said.

His parents faded into the background. Brayden sat beside the gravestone. He traced the engraved name and dates on the smooth marble stone with his finger. She was only alive eleven years. So wrong. He pictured his little sister sitting beside him with her wispy blond hair fluttering in the breeze.

"I really miss you," he said. "It still seems like I'm just having a nightmare, probably from watching too many creepy movies, and that I'll wake up and you'll be in your room writing another story."

A white butterfly fluttered by his face and landed on one of the daisies.

"I read one of your stories. It was from your 'Private Collection,' but I thought maybe now you wouldn't mind."

He imagined her thin arms going to her hips in the indignant stance she often had when he was around.

"I couldn't help it. Sometimes I feel like you're slipping away. Again. I need a way to hang on to you."

Her shimmering arms relaxed and folded into her lap.

"I read the last story you wrote. It made my heart hurt. I'm sorry I was a bulldozer," he told her. "I guess I never really thought about how I made you feel. Or how I made anyone feel."

The wind intensified, plucking the daisies from the vase and scattering them up in the air. Two lifted off the ground and began to spin. Brayden took a deep breath and forced his heart rate to slow down. The daisies settled back to the ground. He gathered them and returned them to the vase.

"Weird little talent I have now, isn't it? I wish I could have controlled the wind the day of the real tornado. I wish I could have saved you."

He watched a woolly caterpillar inch its way through the grass. It found a pink daisy that he failed to pick up and crawled over the petal, settling on a leaf.

"I'm going to be different this year. My bulldozer days are over. I promise."

The wavering image of Willow smiled at him. He imagined her sniffing the daisies and then skipping away on the grass, her white sundress fluttering in the wind.

Mom and Dad were walking back to the car. Their steps were slow and silent, each deep in their own thoughts. Mom's limp seemed more pronounced than usual. Dad reached out and held Mom's hand. When she looked up, she had tears in her eyes. Brayden pushed himself to his feet, took one last look at the tombstone, and followed behind them.

CHAPTER 26

STORM POWER

The alarm buzzed, but Brayden wasn't in bed to silence it. He was already drying off from his shower. Nervous energy coursed through him as he combed his recently cut, wet hair. The mirror fogged up. He wiped the center with his hand so he could see his reflection. The scar on his forehead had faded to a pink line and was partially covered by his hair—unless he made some of the hair spike up with gel. The rest of his outward scars from the tornado were gone. Would everyone have forgotten about the tornado and treat him normal again? Would he slide back into unwanted routines and roles?

"Breakfast!" Mom called.

Brayden buttoned his new shirt, slammed the off button on his alarm clock and drifted downstairs. A whole wheat cinnamon roll and pile of eggs were already on his plate.

"Good morning," Dad said.

"Morning. Hey, Mom. Can I have some frosting for the cinnamon roll?"

"Actually, I'd like you to try it without frosting. It's better for you that way."

"Doesn't the whole wheat flour make it healthy enough?" asked Brayden.

"How can you tell it's whole wheat?"

"It's speckled and darker than the white flour ones."

Mom crinkled her nose. "I was trying to be sneaky. I put in a *little* white flour. Just try it."

Brayden looked at Dad and bit into the cinnamon roll. "It's good."

Mom smiled.

"But it would be even better with a little frosting."

She sighed and got up from the table. "I'll make some for the first day of school, but then we're done with frosting." She mixed powdered sugar and milk in a small bowl and drizzled frosting on Brayden's cinnamon roll.

"Thanks, Mom."

Dad pushed his cinnamon roll forward. "While you're at it, can I have some too?"

Mom put a glob on his roll. "For today *only*."

"Thanks, sweetheart."

Brayden shoveled a spoonful of eggs into his mouth. "Can I drive to school today?"

Dad shook his head. "We've been over this. We only want you driving in emergencies."

"But the doctor said it was probably okay for short distances."

"The doctor doesn't believe you have dizzy spells where you cause tornados. What would happen if you had an episode while driving?" asked Mom. "Biking is much safer."

"The guys will give me a hard time if they find out I still bike to school."

"Then they aren't worthy of having you for a friend," Mom insisted. "Finish your frosted cinnamon roll."

Brayden was soon pedaling his way to school, hoping he was early enough to avoid notice. He locked his bike and entered the front doors. Time for a fresh start. He dug through his backpack until he found his new combination and class schedule. It took three times for him to spin the numbers right on the lock, but he finally opened it and crammed his backpack inside the small space.

"How was your summer?" asked a familiar voice.

Brayden spun around and found himself staring down into Kenzie's blue eyes. She smiled. Was it possible that she was even prettier than he remembered? He suddenly forgot what she asked.

"Hey, Kenzie."

"Hi." She bit her lip, but the corners of her mouth were still curved upwards. "Did you have a good summer?"

That's what she asked. "Not bad. How about you?"

"It was decent. My family and I went to Arizona for a week to visit my grandparents. The rest of the summer I just worked at a frozen yogurt place and hung out with friends. Did you wind up working?"

"I helped Max with his yard business."

"That's good." Her eyes flicked up to his forehead. "How's your head? It sure looks better."

He rubbed the scar self-consciously. "It feels better, too. I mean, on the inside. My head doesn't hurt as much." Why was he having trouble talking?

"I'm so glad." She looked down the hallway and rolled her eyes. Max, Trey, Ian, Parker and Gavin were strutting down the hall. "Looks like the squad is arriving. I'll see you later."

227

"See you." He stared after her until his friends blocked his view.

"Already staking a claim on Kenzie, huh?" Gavin said, pounding Brayden's back. "Way to start the year."

"We were just talking."

"So did you go out this summer?" asked Trey. "You never mentioned her at football practice."

"That's because we didn't go out. This is the first time I've seen her since school ended."

"Maybe I should ask her out," said Ian.

"And what? Take her to your place to help you babysit? Besides, she can't stand you," said Max.

"How do you know? That could have all changed over the summer," Ian said. "This year I'll be able to get any girl I want. Once they see me at our first football game, they'll be fighting over me."

The rest of the guys laughed.

"Go ahead and laugh now, but you'll see. I've been awe-inspiring during practice. Coach told me I'll get lots of time on the field."

"That doesn't mean the girls will notice you," said Trey.

"I have other ways of getting noticed." Ian scanned the hallway. "Check this out." He snatched the hat off a short kid with a buzz cut and tossed it to Parker. "No hats in school."

"Give it back!" the kid squeaked.

"Give it back!" Ian imitated in an exaggerated squeaky voice.

Parker and Ian tossed the hat back and forth over the heads of everyone in the hall.

"Come on," the kid pleaded. "I need to get to class."

"Oh you do? Here. Let me help you look your best." Ian stuck the hat in the drinking fountain and filled it with water.

He jammed the hat on the kid's head. "There you go. Much better."

Ian and Parker laughed as water trickled down the kid's face. More kids joined in the laughter. Brayden felt his head start spinning and debated on what to do. The bell rang and everyone started to shuffle to class.

Brayden concentrated on regulating his breathing and forced the spinning back under control. He scowled as he found his seat in American Literature. Why hadn't he stopped Ian and Parker? They were only a few minutes into the school year, and his friends were already tormenting others.

He looked around the classroom, quickly noting that there weren't any other football players. Two of Kenzie's friends sat near the front talking to each other. Logan sat right behind them, arranging his pens and pencils in a row on his desk. He turned and waved. Brayden waved back in surprise, suddenly reminded that they ended the year on speaking terms.

The teacher, Mrs. Hensley, handed everyone a syllabus for the year, and spent most of the class time discussing it. Brayden discovered his brain could actually focus. What a huge contrast to last May. After three more classes, he was confident that his mind had returned to normal.

Until he walked to lunch. The guys claimed the same table that they used the previous year. They were all sitting down, when Brayden realized his lunch bag only contained an apple.

"Going on a diet?" asked Trey.

"Nah. I think the rest dumped out in my backpack." He grabbed the empty paper sack. "I'll be right back."

He returned to his locker, retrieved his sandwich and some Frito chips and stuffed them back into the bag.

"Hey, kid!" someone yelled.

Brayden turned around. A tall senior grabbed a freshmen's arm as he tried to pass.

"What's your name?" the senior asked.

"Nick. Why?" The freshman tried to pull his arm away.

"Because, Nick, I seem to have forgotten my lunch."

"So?"

"So? You may not realize it, Nick, being new to the school and all, but as a freshman, it's your job to make sure I eat."

"What?"

"I'm hungry. So hand over your food."

Nick yanked on his arm. "You've got to be kidding."

"No, and I don't have all day. I'm sure you don't want punched on your first day of school." The senior pulled back his fist menacingly.

Brayden shook his head. "You can't be serious," he said out loud. He felt a wave of dizziness, but walked toward the pair anyhow. He couldn't just stand by and do nothing yet again.

"Who invited you? Keep walking."

"I will once you let go of his arm," Brayden said, standing his ground. He felt the wind rustle in his hair.

"And I suppose you're going to make me? Did you bring your Mommy to help you?"

"I think I can handle you on my own," Brayden said taking a step closer. He wasn't sure if he was strong enough or even steady enough to pull the senior off Nick, but he decided to try. He lurched forward, but before he could even reach the pair, a gust of wind slammed the senior into the lockers. Brayden felt an instant release of pressure in his head.

Nick's jaw dropped. "I don't know what just happened, but that was awesome." He sped down the hall.

Brayden rushed to the senior, who was now crumpled on the floor. "Are you okay?"

The dazed teen nodded vacantly.

"Do you need help up?"

"No. I think I'll just sit here for a while."

"Okay." Brayden returned to the lunchroom, holding his own lunch to his chest.

"Did you get lost?" asked Gavin. "That took you forever."

"You'd better hurry," said Max. "The bell is going to ring soon."

Brayden nodded and bit into his sandwich. His dizziness was gone but his mind was still whirling. He hadn't meant to take care of the senior with wind, but it worked. Would Willow have been proud to see her big brother protect someone? Could he do it again? Maybe his tornado power could be used for good after all. This sure beat blowing a cat out of a tree.

Parker was talking but Brayden didn't hear a word he said. He was picturing himself walking around the lunchroom, blowing away everyone who was mistreating others. What would he call himself? Did it matter if people knew who he was or did he need a mask?

"Hello? Is anyone home?" asked Parker. "Why do you have that dopey grin on your face?"

Brayden leaned back in his chair, finally focusing on Parker's words. "Sorry. I was just distracted by the wind."

"What wind?"

"The winds of change." Brayden hoped he sounded deep, but after looking at his friends he realized he probably just sounded crazy.

CHAPTER 27

GUST IN THE FACE

The next day, Brayden searched for any sign of cruelty. He patrolled the halls, watching and listening. Out of the corner of his eye, he spotted Logan drop his books. Brayden veered sharply in his direction, scanning the crowd for the bully who knocked them out of his hands. No one was laughing or looked particularly guilty.

"Everything okay?" he asked, bending down to pick up a calculus book and a rainbow assortment of folders.

"Oh. Yes. I just didn't have a firm grip on my books. Thanks."

"No problem."

Brayden continued down the hall. Three girls were comparing schedules. A guy with long hair was digging through his locker searching for the right book. A continual flood of people rushed to class. How surprising to find that everyone seemed to be getting along. He was almost disappointed.

He sat in the back seat in the middle row of U.S. History so he could observe his classmates. Max and Trey sat on either side of him. They actually pulled out paper and pens and took notes like they were instructed. Brayden shrugged and joined in, marveling at how studious they were being. He scanned the rest of the class. No spitballs. No teasing. Occasionally some of them would whisper and a few people were reading notes, but no bullying.

The bell rang. Brayden followed the mob into the hall. He spotted Kenzie at the drinking fountain, holding her long hair out of the water stream.

"Hey, Kenzie," he said.

She looked up in surprise. "Hi. I don't seem to run into you very often. Do we have *any* classes together this year?"

"Just P.E."

"Oh, yeah. How's your day going?"

Brayden paused for a moment. "Good," he finally said.

"You don't seem sure. What's going on?"

"Nothing." Brayden looked over her shoulder, watching the crowd. "Nothing seems to be going on."

Kenzie cocked her head to the side. "Is there something you want to happen?"

"No. I just…it's kind of hard to explain."

"Maybe I can keep up. Go ahead."

The bell rang. Brayden stifled a sigh of relief. "I guess we'd better go. See you in P.E." He hustled down the hallway.

At lunch, the guys at his table joked around and insulted each other, but it never got out of hand. Brayden picked at his plate of nachos.

"Something wrong with your food?" asked Gavin.

Brayden looked up. "No. Why?"

"You aren't actually eating it. Is the cheese more rubbery than usual? Do you need me to eat it for you?" Gavin asked, reaching for the plate.

Brayden pulled the nachos closer. "No. I'm good." He stuffed three cheese-laden chips into his mouth to prove it.

Ian sneezed dramatically all over the table, spraying all of the food, including the nachos.

Max punched his arm. "You just got spit all over my pizza."

"I can't help it. I have allergies or something," Ian said wiping his nose on the back of his hand.

Brayden looked at his nachos in disgust. They glistened with sneeze juice. "Now there really is something wrong with my nachos." He pushed them away.

Gavin grabbed the chips and started eating. The guys grimaced in disgust.

"What can I say? I'm really hungry."

The rest of the group threw their last bits of food in the trash and headed to class. Brayden and Trey took their time walking to the locker room and changing into their gym clothes. When they emerged, most of the class was already dressed and waiting for Coach. Kenzie sat against the wall, talking to several of her friends. She waved. Brayden grinned and waved back.

Maya waddled out of the girl's locker room, trying to pull her shirt further down over her ever-expanding waist. Two girls started laughing.

"Maybe you need to get a bigger size," Sophie said.

"If they even make shirts that big," Victoria replied, laughing.

Maya blushed and lowered her head as she walked past them.

"How much do you think she eats every day?" asked Sophie. "You'd think she would at least try to lose weight."

Brayden's head began to whirl. Good. He wanted to wipe the smirks off their faces. He hoped he could send them spinning out of the room. He raised his hand. A gust of wind blew their perfectly straightened hair into their eyes and caused it to stick up in several places. And then it stopped.

"What was that?" Sophie asked.

"I don't know, but now your hair looks awful," Victoria commented.

"Oh, yeah? Well, so does yours. I need a mirror."

"Me, too."

They ducked back into the locker room. Brayden smacked his head. That was it? His super power messed up their hair. What good would that do? His heart sank. The girls reappeared minutes later with their silky hair almost back in place. He shook his head. They weren't even counted as tardy.

Coach took roll and then made everyone run laps for the beginning-of-the-year physical. Maya was the first to drop out, after jogging and walking for two laps. She had to lean against the wall as she tried to catch her breath.

"Figures," Victoria said as she sprinted past.

Brayden fumed as he ran lap after lap. He hoped his dizziness would return long enough to give the snide girls a better blast, but his head remained clear. The students had to spend the rest of the hour being tested on sit ups, pushups and pull ups. Maya attempted each exercise, but continued to be the first one out. At the end of class, Victoria and Sophie huddled together next to Maya, laughing at her expense.

Brayden raised his hand in one final attempt to silence them, but nothing happened. He gritted his teeth and walked up to Maya. "Your hair looks really good today."

She raised her downcast face in surprise. "Thanks."

Sophie and Victoria stared in shock.

"I noticed you were helping Coach bag up our supplies for football practice. Thanks. We all appreciate it."

"Oh. Sure. I kind of had to drop out of running early, so he asked if I wanted to help."

"I'll bet it put him in a good mood. That will keep him from yelling at us so much after school. Way to go."

Maya smiled. "Glad I could help."

Sophie ran her fingers through her straightened hair and Victoria sucked in her already flat stomach when he looked in their direction. Most guys found them attractive. Too bad all of their beauty was used up on their looks. They were shallow and mean underneath.

"Is it windy today?" he asked, staring at their hair as he walked past.

Maya giggled as they rushed back into the locker room. Brayden showered and changed back into his clothes, still disappointed his power had fizzled when he needed it. Kenzie was waiting for him outside the gym doors and gave him a hug.

"What was that for?" he asked in surprise.

"I heard what you said to Maya. She was so happy she was singing in the shower afterward. And Sophie and Victoria actually left her alone. I've tried getting them to ease up on Maya, but they just tune me out. It drove them nuts today that you complimented Maya instead of them."

Brayden grinned. "Good."

She studied his face. "You impress me sometimes."

"How's that?"

"You don't seem to think about social ranking anymore. I mean, encouraging Maya and putting Sophie and Victoria in their place. That's brave. You're making me reconsider my idea that all football players are egotistical show-offs."

"Thanks?"

Kenzie crossed her arms. "I may actually watch you play this weekend."

236

"Aren't you in band? Don't you always come to our games to play at half time?" asked Brayden. "Or at least in the pep band or something?"

"Yeah. But I usually just talk all the way through it." She blushed. "Sorry, but it's true. I wasn't exactly a huge supporter."

"But now you are? Will you be yelling and whistling whenever I make a great play?"

"Possibly. *If* you make a great play."

Trey snuck up behind Brayden and pounded his back. "With me on the team, he can't help but make a good play. We're going to win every game this season."

"That I would like to see," said Kenzie.

"Then keep your eyes open," Trey bragged. "Come on, Brayden. Coach said we can't have a bunch of tardies on our records this year."

Brayden followed his friend down the hall, turning to wave at Kenzie. She smiled and walked in the opposite direction. He pictured her smile during his remaining classes and on into football practice. His effort intensified as he threw passes and hustled around the field.

"Good effort today," Coach told him.

Brayden nodded.

"Working extra hard, huh?" Trey teased. "You making sure Kenzie likes what she sees on the field tomorrow?"

"You just keep impressing her," Max cut in. "One of her cute friends is actually talking to me now. That whole group was icy last year. Now that you've won Kenzie over, I have a chance."

"Are you sure it's Kenzie you're trying to impress?" asked Ian. "Victoria told me you were being all sweet to Maya. Have you got a thing for big girls now?"

Brayden glared at Ian. "There's nothing wrong with me talking to Maya."

"If you don't care anything about your rep. You upset Victoria and Sophie," Ian continued.

"So? They were teasing Maya."

"They can tease whoever they want. They're the hottest girls in the school," said Ian.

"Maybe to you."

"To almost everyone," Ian insisted. "Just don't mess it up for the rest of us."

"Mess what up?" Brayden asked.

"Don't hurt our chance with good-looking girls just so you can protect the outcasts."

Max stepped in between them. "Hey, would you look at that. We need to get home. See you guys later." He steered Brayden out the doors. "Want a ride?"

"Nah. I've got my bike here."

"Is it locked up?"

"Yes."

"Then leave it. I'll give you a ride tomorrow morning, too. You don't need Ian seeing you bike home right now."

"Good point." He climbed into the truck and let his anger fade during the ride home.

Mom looked up in surprise when Brayden walked through the front door. "You're home early. Did practice go okay?"

"Yeah. Max just gave me a ride." Brayden held up his hand before Mom could question him. "Don't worry about my bike. It's locked up. Max is going to give me a ride tomorrow morning too. I just needed to get away from Ian."

"Anything you want to tell me about?"

"We just don't agree on anything now." He sniffed the air. "What's cooking?"

"Quinoa with mixed vegetables."

"Should I know what quinoa is?"

"I think maybe I made it once before."

"Is it healthy?"

"Yes."

"Did I like it?"

"Well…Maybe not the way I fixed it last time. But I think you'll like the way I made it today. Go ahead and wash up. Dad will be home any minute, and then we can eat."

Banjo followed Brayden to the bathroom sink, wagging his tail. Brayden wrestled with him before washing his hands. The beagle licked him thoroughly.

"I hope you're hungry tonight," Brayden whispered. "I may be slipping you some dinner."

CHAPTER 28

TORNADO MAGNET

The first game of the season was about to begin. Brayden adjusted his helmet and scanned the crowd. The stands were packed more than usual, and a good portion of them wore silver and green. Cougar colors. That didn't usually happen on away games. His parents stood and waved at him. For a brief moment, he wondered where Willow was. She always came to his games, usually waving pom poms while she cheered. Wind whipped through the bleachers, smacking at hats and hair, reminding him that Willow was gone.

"Go, Brayden!" Dad yelled. "Go, Cougars!"

Brayden waved. He was glad his parents were there, but hoped Dad wouldn't embarrass him. The band congregated on the left side of the stands, wearing their green band uniforms. He searched for Kenzie, spotting her in the second row, surrounded by several of her friends. Her long hair was piled into a messy bun on the top of her head. She waved her flute at him.

The whistle blew and his focus returned to the game. Parker mishandled a snap, and the Tiger's linebacker pounced on the loose ball. Soon the opposing team made a touchdown. Some sloppy play followed and Brayden found himself thrown to the ground. Three guys landed on top of him, pinning his arm in a painful position and knocking the wind out of his lungs. He groaned and tried to inhale. A whistle was blown and the guys tumbled off. Brayden swung his sore arm back and forth.

Coach called him to the side lines. "You okay? Did you hit your head?"

"No. My arm's just sore."

"Let's have you sit out for a while just in case. I'm on strict orders to protect your head because of your concussion."

Brayden reluctantly sat on the bench, eager to get back on the field. He grabbed his Gatorade and swished some around in his mouth, energized by the sweetness. His arm ached but he wanted to keep playing. He glanced up into the bleachers. Kenzie was watching the game, chanting a cheer with the crowd. The first comeback was a 10-yard touchdown pass by their senior running back. The crowd screamed. They forced a punt but it was downed at the 1-yard line. A penalty was called on Gavin for holding.

"You're up," Coach said.

Brayden jammed his helmet back on, grateful to be back in the game. He immediately blocked a muscle-bound senior from the Tigers. Trey intercepted a pass in the end zone and the crowd began to yell louder. Ian managed to slip unnoticed out of the backfield and behind the opposing team's secondary, where Max connected with him on a 79-yard touchdown.

By halftime, their team was ahead 32-6. They ran off the field pumped up and confident. Brayden paused by the door. For the first time, he actually wished he could watch the marching band during their halftime show. He searched for Kenzie as the band marched onto the field to the beat of the drum section. It wasn't easy to recognize anyone when they had their identical hats on.

"Hurry it up," the manager said.

Brayden frowned but turned to join the team, just as the band began to play Michael Jackson's "Thriller". Coach gave them a pep talk, wrote a few new plays on his whiteboard and hustled them back through the doors. The band had already returned to the stands and was playing the school song as the football players returned to the field.

Only minutes into the second half of the game, Ian scored a second touchdown. Brayden was glad their lead was extended but knew Ian would be full of himself the next week at school. A snap over the punter's head led to a field goal. Brayden blocked a punt that resulted in yet another touchdown for his team. The crowd performed a silver and green wave in response. Even Kenzie joined in. The Tigers returned an interception for a touchdown of their own. Parker scored from 1-yard out with just under three minutes remaining to lock in a win for the Cougars.

The entire team bounced off each other, hyped up from winning the first game of the season. Coach released a huge belly laugh. The fans were yelling and the band played the school song over and over. Brayden's mom and dad were yelling his name and whistling. Brayden looked for Kenzie but saw she was being herded with the rest of the band toward the buses. He felt like he was swimming against the current trying to reach her.

"Kenzie," he called.

She was too far away to hear him over the crowd. He weaved his way through the masses, grateful he still had on shoulder pads.

"Kenzie!" he called again.

She was distracted and did not turn around. Her hands were on her hips as she yelled at two guys in Cougar football uniforms. "That isn't funny. Give him back his saxophone!"

"Or what?" Ben asked.

"Or it could break," she said. "Not everything is as indestructible as a football."

"We'll give it back when he learns his place. He told some guys from the Tigers that he was sorry they lost." Ben tossed the saxophone to his buddy again.

"Because we grew up together," yelled the saxophone player. "I can say what I want."

"Then we can play what we want. And right now we want to play *Toss the Sax*."

Brayden felt his head spin. Would it fizzle out before he could help? Ben threw the saxophone too hard and it went beyond the reach of his buddy. Kenzie gasped. Brayden reached out his hand and a gust of wind blew under the saxophone, suspending it in the air. It began to spin, but kept well above the ground. Everyone nearby gawked at it in silence.

"What in the world…" Ben began.

Kenzie approached the saxophone cautiously and pulled it from the tiny tornado. She handed it to the owner. He quickly began checking the keys and played a scale on it to be sure it still worked.

"Thanks, Kenzie," he said. He rushed past the football players and boarded the bus.

Ben turned to Brayden. "Did you see that? Was that a freaky bit of wind or what?"

"Yeah. Hey, Coach wants us to start getting on our own bus."

The two seniors nodded, still in shock over the spinning saxophone. They turned and left.

Kenzie was staring at Brayden. "Did you have anything to do with that?"

Brayden flushed. "What do you mean?"

"That saxophone should have fallen to the ground," she said, studying his face. "How could it suddenly start spinning like that? It was almost as if it was in a tornado."

"Pretty strange, huh?"

"Kind of a coincidence that a survivor of a tornado arrives just in time for a mini-tornado to protect someone's instrument."

"I must be a tornado magnet," Brayden said.

"Yeah. Something like that."

Brayden envisioned the wheels turning in her head. He debated on whether to just explain everything, but he wasn't sure how she would react.

"Good game, by the way," she said.

Brayden smiled, grateful she was letting it go. "I noticed you were watching this time."

She shrugged. "It's actually interesting when there's someone worth watching on the team."

"Yeah, Ian did a good job," Brayden said with a crooked grin.

She snorted. "Ian. I guess he knows how to play, but I doubt I'll ever be an Ian fan."

"Oh. So you liked watching Gavin?"

"You're hilarious."

"Parker?"

"Keep it up, and I won't actually watch you next time."

Marissa walked up behind them. "We're loading the buses now. Come on, Kenzie."

Kenzie let her friend pull her to the bus. "Bye. And thanks for helping with the saxophone," she said, looking over her shoulder.

"You bet." Brayden almost dropped his helmet. "I mean, with what little I did." Did he just give himself away? What exactly was she thinking?

The crowd parted around him as he joined the other guys, still cheering as they crammed onto a bus of their own. The air reeked of sweat and diesel fumes, but the excitement was contagious.

Ian smacked Brayden on the shoulder pads. "Two touchdowns! I told you Coach would give me lots of time on the field. Did you hear everyone yelling for me?"

"For you and the rest of the team," said Brayden.

"Yeah," Max added. "You did notice that the rest of us were out there with you, right?"

"Sure. It would have been harder to score on my own."

"Try impossible to score on your own," corrected Trey.

"Who cares?" said Gavin. "We won!"

The rest of the guys started chanting, "Cougars! Cougars! Cougars!" They continued chanting and cheering for the entire bus ride back to South High School.

Brayden hoped that by Monday, Ian's gloating would fade. Not a chance.

"Great touchdowns," a classmate said.

"I know, right?" Ian answered. He and Parker strutted down the hall. Brayden and Max followed close behind. Ian stopped at a pretty sophomore cheerleader's locker and crossed his arms in a way that displayed his biceps. "So, what did you think of Friday's game?"

"That was so exciting! I'm glad we won. Were you there?" she asked.

Parker snickered.

"I'm on the team," Ian said, dumbfounded.

"Oh. That's good. Did you see me cheering? It was my first game. I think I nailed my routine."

Ian gripped her locker door, looking like he wanted to shake her. "I scored two touchdowns."

"Hey. Good for you. I did a roundoff after each touchdown. Maybe you saw me."

Max and Brayden saw Ian's expression and tried not to laugh.

"No, I was too busy winning the game," he spat out as he walked back to his friends. "Can you believe her?"

"You two would be perfect for each other," said Max.

Ian scowled, elbowing anyone who did not clear a path as he barreled through the crowd. A scrawny boy with a limp stopped suddenly in the middle of the hall. He was deep in thought and didn't see the group of football players approaching. They had to stop short.

"Move it, loser," Ian said.

The kid looked up with a puzzled expression.

"See? He knows his name," Ian continued. "Loser! You're in our way."

"Knock it off, Ian," Brayden said.

"Why? No one blocks us."

"We don't own the hallways," Brayden insisted. His head started to spin.

"Yeah, I think we do. Especially after last Friday night. When we make our team win, we make the whole school look good. We deserve respect. *I* deserve respect."

The kid didn't move. He looked down at his feet instead and started rocking back and forth.

"Why are you still standing there, Loser?" asked Ian.

"I don't know you," the kid said.

Ian glared at him. "If you had gone to the game like any normal student, you would know exactly who I am. I'm the one who scored two touchdowns. Get a clue." Ian pushed the kid out of his way.

"Don't push me."

Ian turned, his face darkening. He grabbed the kid's shirt under his neck. "What did you say?"

"Let him go," Brayden said. He raised his hand, ready to blow him away.

"Or what?" Ian sneered. "And what's with the hand?"

Brayden squinted, trying to release a tornado. Nothing happened. Disappointment washed over him. Why couldn't he get better control over his power? Only getting it to work half of the time just wasn't good enough. He lowered his hand but stepped forward. "Just leave him alone."

"Are you joining the loser club now, too? Did that tornado screw up your brain for good?" He started to lift the kid up by his shirt.

Max stepped up beside Brayden. "Put the kid down and cool off."

"You two really want to get into it over this loser? He's not worth it."

A girl ran over to them. "Martin? Why aren't you in the Resource Room? Your para is looking for you."

"I c-c-can't." He pointed helplessly to Ian's hand.

"Sure you can." Brayden said. "Ian's letting go now."

Ian dropped him, rolling his eyes. "I didn't know he was a…"

The girl clamped her hand over Ian's mouth. "Nice guy? That's right, you didn't." She smiled reassuringly at the boy, who was rocking again. "Go on to class, Martin." Her eyes followed him until he entered the right door, then she uncovered Ian's mouth. She was almost as tall as Ian and stood within inches of his face. "You have no idea how much damage you could do calling him a name. He would repeat it for months. It's going to be hard enough getting 'loser' out of his head. If I ever catch you hurting or insulting my little brother again, I will make sure you're suspended. He has enough to handle without a thug like you boosting your own inflated ego at his expense." She turned to Brayden and Max. "Thanks for trying to help."

The bell rang. She glared at Ian and stalked off.

"She told you," Parker commented.

Ian frowned. "Shut up."

Brayden chuckled as they separated to get to their classes. A tornado would have been more exciting, but a tongue lashing was good, too. At least Ian seemed to get the message.

CHAPTER 29

WIND CHIMES

Weeks passed and Brayden gained confidence in thwarting bullying attempts. Sometimes he was able to emit wind to help his cause, but he found that his words were just as effective—and didn't require an explanation.

He often stopped by Kenzie's lunch table so they could walk to P.E. together. Every once in a while, she would join him at his table instead. Brayden's friends didn't mind, because she was usually accompanied by Marissa, Lindsay and Tosha. The guys stumbled over each other trying to impress them.

"Does anyone need a ride to the parade this weekend?" asked Max, looking directly at Marissa. "My dad said I can drive his truck."

"Or if you want to ride in style, you can come with me in my car," said Ian.

"I could use a ride," Parker said. "My car is in the shop."

"Yeah, okay. Anyone else?" None of the girls responded. Ian's lip curled. "Are you driving to the parade, Brayden? Oh, wait. You aren't driving yet, are you?

Mommy and Daddy are still afraid to let you behind the wheel. I guess you could bike there. You still bike to school every day, don't you?"

Brayden resisted the urge to kick Ian under the table. "Biking makes me the fine physical specimen you see today."

"I didn't know you still biked to school," Kenzie said.

"Pathetic, right?" asked Ian. He laughed through his beaked nose.

"Actually, I bike to school most days, too," Kenzie stated. "I used to bike with a neighbor friend, but she graduated last year. I'd rather not bike alone."

Brayden smiled. "We could bike together on days when I don't have football practice after school. Your house isn't much out of my way."

"You know where she lives?" teased Trey. "Are you some kind of stalker or something?"

Brayden felt the heat flood his neck and he dropped his head. "I just looked it up one time."

Now it was Kenzie's turn to smile. "I think that's sweet."

"That's sweet all right," said Ian, pretending to gag. He crumpled up his lunch sack and threw it in the trash.

"Aww. Don't be mad," said Max. "Sometimes your attempts to humiliate just don't turn out like you hope."

"Yeah," Brayden said. "I owe you one." He and Kenzie started walking to class. When they turned the corner he stopped. "Can I meet you at the bike rack today? We have the night off from football."

Her eyes sparkled as she smiled and nodded.

Maya was standing outside the girl's locker room, staring at the door. Kenzie cleared her throat. Maya jumped.

"Oh, hi, Kenzie. Hi, Brayden."

"Are you going in?" asked Kenzie.

"Yeah. Some days it just takes a little psyching up. Changing into gym clothes is hard enough, but add Sophie and Victoria to it…well…"

"Let's walk in together," Kenzie suggested. She waved to Brayden.

He waved and then sucked in a mouthful of fresh air before plunging into the boy's locker room. His personal challenge was to only inhale five times while in the smelly room. His fingers whirled through his combination and he pulled out his gym shirt.

"Hey, Brayden?" Miguel called as he tied his shoes. "My aunt said two guys named Max and Brayden took care of her yard this summer. Were you the Brayden she was talking about?"

"Probably. Who's your aunt?"

"Aunt Campos. She has an annoying Chihuahua named Pico."

"Yeah. I remember him." Brayden gave up restricting his breath intake. The sweat smell washed over him.

"She got a new job, and is gone in the afternoons. She wants me to walk Pico each day after school."

Brayden grimaced. "Have fun with that."

Miguel shook his head. "The thing is, I can't even get the leash on his collar. He snarls and bites whenever I get close."

"That sounds about right."

"My aunt said I should get advice on how to handle him from you. She said Pico actually seemed to like you. How did you manage that?"

"I don't know if *like* is the right word. Maybe you could bribe him with dog treats when you put his leash on. That way his mouth would be busy chewing the treat, not you."

251

Miguel shrugged. "Worth a try. Thanks."

"No problem."

Brayden rushed out into the gym, grateful to breathe fresher air. Coach took role and then reviewed the finer points of playing basketball. He divided them into four teams and the games began.

Brayden was disappointed that Kenzie wasn't on his team. He was curious about her basketball skills, and knew he could hold his own on the court.

Miguel, Brayden and a girl he didn't recognize worked together well, passing the ball back and forth, shooting baskets often. Victoria stood to the side looking bored. Maya gave up running after the ball and waited by the basketball hoop.

Coach walked by. Victoria rolled her eyes and joined the game. She managed to steal the ball from another player and dribbled it across the court.

"Pass it to Maya. She's open," Brayden said.

"Are you kidding?" Victoria snapped.

An opposing player snatched the ball from her hands and scored. Miguel dribbled it back across the court. Maya held her arms open. Miguel paused for a moment and tossed her the ball. She caught it and tossed it into the basket.

Brayden and his teammates, with the exception of Victoria, cheered. Maya patted herself on the back.

"Well done," Coach said.

By the time class was over, Brayden had sweat circles under his arm pits. He took a whiff of his shirt and decided now was not the best time to talk to Kenzie. He eagerly waited until the final bell of the day rang, and then headed to the bike rack.

Kenzie was already standing by her bike. She smiled when she saw him and strapped on her helmet. She stuffed a few stray wisps of hair into the sides. "Ready?"

He jammed on his own helmet, glad it no longer hurt his head. "Yep. Let's go."

They walked their bikes until they passed the first crosswalk and then pedaled down the sidewalk. Brayden found himself grinning as he followed Kenzie. Her dark hair billowed behind her in the breeze. A bug smacked into his teeth. He spit it out and kept his mouth shut until they reached the first stoplight.

Brayden pushed the button to cross. They waited side by side as cars zipped past.

"Thanks for biking with me," Kenzie said.

"You bet."

She chewed her lip for a moment, looking into his brown eyes. "You've really changed."

"I have?"

She nodded.

"Is that good or bad?"

"Definitely good. Last year you were so…arrogant. You didn't seem to care about anyone else. At least, not until the end of the year. You know, after the tornado." She blushed. "Sorry. That's not exactly a great thing to say on our first bike ride together."

He shrugged. "Don't worry about it. It's true."

"So why the change?"

The blinking countdown light flashed three, two, one.

"Oops," Kenzie said. "We missed it." She pushed the button again.

"Actually, do you want to sit on the grass while we wait again?" asked Brayden.

She nodded. They walked their bikes off the sidewalk and sat under a tree. The breeze was in a frisky mood and played with Kenzie's hair, blowing it across her face. She brushed it aside.

"You asked about the change. Are you sure you want to know?"

"Yes."

Brayden ran his fingers through the grass, mustering up the courage to speak. "You heard about my little sister dying in the tornado."

Kenzie nodded.

"She was always writing and illustrating little stories. Most of them were in this purple notebook she carried around. I read one of the stories." He swallowed. "It had me in it. I was a bulldozer. She was a bug car and I crushed her." His throat tightened. "It got me thinking about how I treated her. How I treated everybody. I don't want to be a bulldozer now."

Kenzie reached over and held his hand. "Willow would love how you've changed. You're not a bulldozer anymore. You're more like a cool camaro."

Brayden soaked in her words and savored the feeling of her hand in his.

"Have you read any of her other stories?" she asked.

He shook his head. "I guess I didn't want to read about anything else I did to hurt her."

"Maybe it's not all bad."

"Maybe."

Silence stood between them for several minutes. Not an awkward silence, but one that felt peaceful…comforting. The cars that sped past seemed like they were from another world. He inhaled the scent of grass and pine bark, enjoying the moment. He stroked Kenzie's hand with his thumb.

"The crossing light is blinking again," he said with a grin.

"We've missed it several times."

"Guess we should get you home."

"Yeah."

They both sat for another minute or two until a horn blared down the street. Reluctantly, they got back on their bikes and pedaled to Kenzie's house. They waved good-bye and Brayden continued home.

"That took a little longer than usual," Mom said. "Did you think you had practice tonight and end up going to the field?"

"No. I found out Kenzie doesn't have anyone to bike home with anymore. I figured on the nights I don't have practice, I could bike with her. It's not very safe for a girl to bike by herself."

Mom's eyebrows shot up. "That's nice of you to be concerned about her safety. Seems like the name Kenzie pops up in your conversation quite often."

Brayden shrugged. "It's possible."

"I looked her up in your yearbook the last time you mentioned her. She was pictured in lots of clubs and in the band. She's pretty."

"Yeah, I guess."

"Homecoming is next month, isn't it?"

"I suppose."

"Girls usually like going to those things."

"Mom!"

"I'm just saying…"

Brayden rolled his eyes and escaped upstairs. He didn't want to admit it, but Homecoming might not be a bad idea this year. He walked past Willow's room. The door was open. His eyes drifted to the purple notebook on her desk.

255

Maybe Kenzie was right. There could be some stories that wouldn't be painful to read. He debated in the doorway for a few minutes. Finally, he reached for the notebook and sat on Willow's bed. He kicked off his shoes so he wouldn't get her bedspread dirty and leaned back on her pillows. He stroked the notebook's cover, imagining Willow using her markers to draw the puffy letters in the words *Private Collection*. This time, he started from the beginning.

The first story was about a penguin, shy and nervous about going to school on the iceberg for the first time. He studied the illustration and recognized the shirt the penguin wore as one of Willow's favorites. There were several stories about Banjo and his misadventures. She included a picture of him eating a jar of Vaseline that he pulled off the bathroom counter. Brayden laughed, remembering the incident. Banjo barked like a seal for weeks afterwards. There was a story about a unicorn that was teased because his horn was crooked. Had she ever been teased about her crooked tooth or was this just a random story? Another story was about a family of rabbits. Their mom made them a healthy vegetable loaf that wound up coming to life and chasing them around the house.

Eventually, he came to a story he recognized. There was a picture of two mice flying kites. The smaller mouse wore a neon pink panda shirt. He held the picture closer. One kite was filled with purple, pink and green butterflies. The other had footballs and a misshapen gecko. He recalled the day she wrote that story, and remembered being awful to her that morning. He braced himself for some painful reading.

Once there were two mice named Frieda and Frederick. They lived in a cozy mouse house with their mom and dad.

The wind often shook their little house, making it moan and groan.

"Oh, that noisy wind," complained her mom.

"Oh, that destructive wind," grumbled her dad.

One day, Frieda decided the wind must be blowing their house because it was lonely. She went outside and threw leaves in the air. The wind swirled the leaves around her. It was fun. That night the wind left their house alone.

Several days passed, and the wind shook their little house, making it moan and groan.

"Oh, that noisy wind," complained her mom.

"Oh, that destructive wind," grumbled her dad.

Frieda went outside with her scarf. The wind swirled the scarf around her. It was fun. That night the wind left their house alone.

Several days passed, and the wind shook their little house, making it moan and groan.

"Oh, that noisy wind," complained her mom.

"Oh, that destructive wind," grumbled her dad.

Frieda sat down and made a kite. She drew flowers all over it and colored them in. She was about to go outside, when she thought about her brother, Frederick. He might want to fly a kite too. She drew footballs and a gecko on his kite and carried it to his room.

"What's that?" he asked in his grumpy voice.

"A kite."

"What's on it? Mud and a moldy burrito?"

"No. Footballs and a gecko."

"Great. Now leave."

Frieda's heart hurt. "But can't we go fly kites together with the wind?"

"No. High schoolers don't do that. Now go."

Frieda was sad, but went outside to play with the wind. They had fun, but she couldn't get her kite in the air, and she missed her brother. Suddenly, Frederick appeared holding his kite.

"Would you like help?" he asked.

"Yes, please."

He helped her over and over until her kite was flying high in the air. Then Frederick started flying the kite she made for him. Both kites soared up and down. Frieda and Frederick laughed and laughed. The wind was having so much fun it almost blew her away.

"Be careful. You're so scrawny the wind might blow you higher than your kite," said Frederick.

"Then you'd better fly with your kite and save me," Frieda answered.

The wind smiled, and blew so hard that Frieda was swept up into the sky. Frederick flew right up after her. They had the best day ever. From then on, the wind only blew when he wanted the two mice to come out to play. Mom quit complaining. Dad quit grumbling. And their mouse house was a happy place. The End.

Brayden closed the notebook, unsure of whether to laugh or cry. He gently returned the notebook to her desk and walked to his room. He pushed books off his desk, revealing the kite with the footballs and gecko. Tears threatened his eyes, but he ignored them and stepped outside.

Cars were driving by. Kids were playing on their front lawns. He didn't care. Protecting a false image was a waste of time. He uncoiled the long string and started running down the sidewalk. This time, the kite rose and fell in a gentle rhythm behind him. The wind blew a steady stream of air, keeping the kite floating above the treetops. He pictured

Willow running at his side, her blue eyes sparkling and her mouth stretched into a smile. The wind chimes played their melodic song in the trees, reminding him of her laugh. He chuckled in unison. The bulldozer was gone. And the wind was happy.